LETTERS FROM

CELL NO. 73

NATHAN W. TUCKER

InArena Publishing House

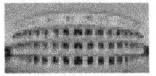

Letters from Cell No. 73 is a work of fiction. Names, characters, places, and incidents are the products of the author's imagination or are used fictitiously. Any resemblance to actual events, locales, or persons, living or dead, is entirely coincidental.

ISBN: 978-0615805771

InArena Publishing House

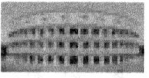

Dedicated to those who do not wish
to see this story written.

LETTER I

MY DEAREST GRANDCHILDREN,

I hope the news has already reached you, but I wanted to tell you myself that I am alive and am treated well enough as a prisoner of war. I hope to see you soon so that we may comfort each other over the loss of your father and my only child. Jonathan was a courageous and fierce soldier who died bravely so that you and your generation may experience a new awakening of freedom in America that has not existed in my lifetime.

You can be proud knowing he died with honor, and by his sacrifice saved many lives, including my own. Our lines were collapsing and we were about to be overrun when Jonathan mounted the machine gun turret and held the enemy at bay until we were able

1

to retreat. His gun was finally silenced by mortar fire, but not until he had saved hundreds of lives by his actions. Knowing your father, I have no doubt that he died with your names on his lips and heart.

Until I see you again face to face, I hope to be able to write you about the mistakes of the past so that your generation may be spared repeating them in the future. If you heed them, you have the opportunity to shape the future so that your own grandchildren may live free from the specter of statism and socialism.

I hope that my letters will find their way to you. Naturally, they don't provide prisoners of war with mail service, so I have resorted to smuggling them out. I realize that in this age of electronic communication and the death of the post office, none of you have likely received an actual paper letter before. I hope you grow to love the feel of the written word on paper as I do, and please keep these letters secret until my men and I are safely released.

With much love and prayers until I can write (or see you) again.

Your affectionate grandfather,
Col. Peter Iossi

LETTER II

MY DEAREST GRANDCHILDREN,

I apologize for not having written sooner. Paper and ink are in short supply in prison, and it can take days or weeks before I can procure more. Life as a prisoner of war is tolerable enough, and fortunately my men and I have not been physically abused or tortured.

Still, one misses the little things that bring joy to life. The blue sky aglow with the sun's warm rays. The comfort of one's own bed at night. The luxuries of air conditioning in the summer and heat in the winter. And the sounds of joy and laughter, which this stone monument to man's illusionary belief in "rehabilitating" criminal offenders has all but silenced.

We are being housed with other prisoners of war at the former federal ADMAX prison in Florence, Colorado, the only supermax prison the federal government had. While known to tourists for its proximity to the Royal Gorge, it managed to become home to thirteen state and federal prisons. Relieved of the need to build any prisons of their own, the Mexican government released the criminals to make space for all the POWs of this Second Mexican-American War. Needless to say, no one but the guards and their families live in Florence and its environs any more.

A former ADMAX warden once described the place as "a cleaner version of Hell." That probably would have been a charitable description in his time. The prison is not yet filthy, though that day is rapidly approaching. The toilets work, most of the time, and when they do not, the halls outside the cell doors become a necessary substitute.

The showers do not work at all, which would be bad enough if confined in solitary as the rooms were originally intended. Instead, the stench becomes unbearable when the seven by twelve foot cell is shared by three, sometimes four, prisoners. Once in a great while they will take us, floor by floor, outside to be hosed off and given new prison uniforms.

Though these often occur in the extremes of nature, I eagerly look forward to these precious few caresses by God's creation.

Each cell was equipped with a black and white television, but those were given as parting gifts to the original inhabitants as they were evicted. There is a four-inch by four-foot window in each cell, but the new warden saw fit to fill them in with brick. The only light we enjoy is the artificial light from the hallways and, in some of the cells, working ceiling fixtures. The light in my cell works, though they never turn it off, leaving us in a world in which notions such as day or night become increasingly meaningless.

Taste is also another gift of God that has no meaning in ADMAX. The only hydration we receive comes from the water fountain built into the toilet. I would have been skeptical of its purity under the best of conditions, and try not to let my mind wonder to its deteriorating state of contamination under current prison management. It has yet to smell or taste funny, but its coloring leaves much to be desired.

To call the food Mexican, or even Tex-Mex, would be an insult to those cuisines. Dinner often consists of Spanish rice, meat of unknown origins (probably best that way) in a tortilla shell, and what the cook calls baked beans. No one touches the beans. Not after that first night. Not ever again. Breakfast is often burnt toast and porridge, while supper usually consists of peanut butter and jelly sandwiches. Sometimes they forget either the peanut butter or the jelly, or both. It makes no difference. Nothing has any taste anymore. We no longer eat for pleasure, but only because we must to survive.

Hope is the only food in this place. The thought of one day seeing your beautiful faces once again strengthens and nourishes me more than any food possibly could. My picture of you was confiscated long ago, but the memory of you is seared on my heart's photo album. It is with all sincerity that I can tell you that you are constantly in my thoughts and prayers.

Despite the nauseating aroma of unwashed bodies, I am thankful for the three soldiers who share Cell No. 73 with me. Solitary confinement, without television, books, sunlight, or a sense of time, would have driven many of us mad within the first weeks of our stay. There is little for us to do but share stories and play games with homemade cards, but it is enough to make each day bearable.

We are kept in lockdown twenty-three hours a day, only leaving our cells for one hour in the exercise room with others on our cell block. There isn't much exercise equipment to speak off, which is just as well given that our diets do not enable much physical activity. Most of us try to maintain a daily regiment of pushups, sit-ups, pull ups, and jumping jacks, but the number of repetitions we can do is steadily decreasing. We pretend not to notice, but our once-impressive military physiques are slowly turning into mere skin and bone.

But while exercise is becoming less of a priority during our daily excursions, camaraderie, and scheming, are. We play games, have a prayer service, and plan. Planning for what, we're not sure, but our training has instilled in us a second nature to prepare a plan of action for any eventuality. Hence we have developed a rudimentary smuggling operation whereby we can sneak things such as letters out, and things crudely called weapons in.

The language barrier with our captors have not proven to be a difficulty. I was one class short of a minor in Spanish in college, and used to be able to read it nearly fluently. Now, alas, I can no longer understand it either written or spoken. They say immersion is the best way to learn a foreign language, but I don't believe they meant placement as a prisoner of war. Our guards almost never say a word to us, but merely watch us with bored disinterest from their stations.

They show little emotion towards us other than mild disdain, except for the Hispanics among us. Though some of them are third or fourth generation Americans, our captives gaze upon them with a hatred reserved for traitors. The Hispanic–Americans avoid any eye contact with the guards for fear that the palpable loathing would translate into physical violence. So far the animosity remains below the boiling point, but we fear that even the slightest incident will set it off.

To my surprise, our captors have no interest in interrogating myself or anyone under my command other than our initial intake interview. Considering that my regiment was the last real military threat to their presence in Colorado, it appears likely that the Mexicans have concluded that their victory is secure and that my interrogation would be neither necessary nor productive.

Our forces had made it as far as the outskirts of Denver and were nearly in control of its airport before being met by a wave of Mexican reinforcements from Arizona. We fought for three days to hold our position against overwhelming odds, but were finally forced to retreat towards the border.

My regiment retreated south, taking up our position just west of Boise City in the Oklahoma Panhandle in hopes of defeating, or at least stalling, these reinforcements before they joined the Mexican armies already battling in Texas. The remainder of our division moved northeast to secure our lands there in the event that Mexico was more greedy than she claimed.

Several thousand of my men died the day our forces clashed in that narrow strip of Oklahoma. After our line faltered, we fought a bitter rearguard action all the way to the border with Texas. We gave as good as we got, but finally had nothing left to give. By nightfall I had no choice but to raise the white flag of surrender as the remaining two-hundred men with me found ourselves surrounded by a sea of armed Mexicans.

I am left to fear how the war goes in Texas, but am glad for your sakes that the Mexican army did not decide to invade our lands to its northeast. I am thankful that I can go to bed each night (or day) knowing that you are safe back home in Iowa. There are rumors of a pending prisoner exchange, so I am hopeful that I may soon join you there. But they are only rumors, so I hesitate to place much confidence in them.

I must close this letter as I have run out of paper. Please DO NOT try to respond to my letters, as they will never reach my eyes and will only serve to alert the prison authorities that we are communicating with the outside.

I do have a small favor to ask of you. It would bring me great joy if you would (temporarily) adopt my black lab Lucky. Since your grandma's death he has been cared for by friends on base, but I would feel much better if he were with family. I know he always enjoys being able to stretch his legs on your acreage.

With much love and prayers until I can write (or see you) again.

Your affectionate grandfather,
Col. Peter Iossi

LETTER III

MY DEAREST GRANDCHILDREN,

In many ways these letters will be my memoirs, for the fall of America occurred in my lifetime, though its seeds were planted long ago. In 1978, I was born in the post-constitutional social democracy called the United States of America, though few recognized it for what it actually was. We were content with the illusion that we were vastly different from the Soviet Union and our distant cousins in Western Europe.

I grew up in Sioux City, where Iowa bordered both Nebraska and South Dakota. The Missouri River, or the "Mighty Mo" as the locals called it, divided Sioux City from South Sioux City, Nebraska, and the Big Sioux River separated the city from North Sioux City in South Dakota. Little Sioux City lay to the south, while Sioux Center and Sioux Falls were north of us. Originality in naming cities was not our forte.

Barges laden with goods, rather than recreational boating, were the most common form of river traffic on the Missouri. Even if one wanted to, swimming in the muddy, polluted river was discouraged due to its dangerous and shifting undercurrents. While there were those who tried their hand at fishing in the Mighty Mo, most never did, opting, like my family, to enjoy the opportunities afforded by nearby lakes.

Though growing up in a metropolitan area of approximately 100,000, Siouxland, as we called the greater tristate region, was very rural and western in feel. Farmers were our neighbors, pickup trucks were in great abundance, rodeos and county fairs were big events, and cowboy hats and boots, while not necessarily in fashion, were certainly not out of fashion.

Adding to its western atmosphere was its sizable Native American populations, both in the city itself and on neighboring reservations. Despite its namesake, the Sioux Indian tribe was nowhere to be found in the city's vicinity. Instead, both the Winnebago and Omaha tribes had reservations just to the south on both sides of the Missouri River.

Both tribes built casinos during my childhood near

Interstate 29, the highway that roughly followed the course of the river south to the Missouri state border. Despite getting rich in the process, the standard of living on the reservations saw little improvement. Growing up, the poverty-filled reservations were my first experience with the effects a welfare state has on its citizens—living conditions more akin to those south of the border than anything else seen in Siouxland.

As a former Secretary of the Interior in the Reagan Administration once noted, the failures of socialism can be poignantly and tragically seen in life on the reservation. But rather than learning from such mistakes, Americans of both political parties heedlessly pursued the same policies on a national scale that inevitably made the country one giant reservation of poverty. Sadly, it often takes the cold, hard fist of reality rather than the experience of others to break the voters' addiction to other people's money.

Contrary to popular opinion, most Iowa families, mine included, did not farm, though there was no escaping the enormous social and economic influence of agriculture on our community. Both my parents had been raised on farms and, while most of our family members no longer worked the land, the family farm was something idealized and treasured. The rugged individualism, self-sufficiency, industry built on hard work, earthen realism, and the cultivation of God's creation were all characteristics to be applauded. Unfortunately, modern agriculture became known for another, more ugly characterization as it became one of the most influential and fattened constituencies of the modern welfare state.

I grew up in a conservative, Christian, middle-class family that did things the old-fashioned way. We went to church Sunday morning, Sunday evening, and Wednesday nights. We ate meals together and had family devotions together. We lived within our means and rarely spent money on such frivolities as eating out, movies, toys, etc. In a remarkable feat of financial stewardship, my parents did not owe anyone anything. The house was paid for, the car notes had long ago been paid off, and my parents were busy saving for college for my siblings and I. Sadly, this Rockwellian picture was not the norm while I was growing up, and was increasing scoffed at by future generations.

Though born during the Carter Administration, Reagan, thankfully, is the first president I can remember. Though I grew up without either grandfather, Reagan in a way became a surrogate television grandfather with his worn but wise face, twinkling eyes, ready and sincere smile, and trusting and comforting voice. Despite all the praise heaped upon President Obama's oratory, it is but amateurish compared with Reagan's gravely baritone that spoke to you as a fellow citizen rather than a celebrity, god-like political savior.

I remember when the Challenger space shuttle exploded in the mid-1980s. I was in school at the time, and the teacher had the bright idea to bring in a television so that we could watch the launch. What was a great experience full of wonder and amazement turned abruptly and horribly wrong seconds after takeoff. Whatever platitudes my teacher tried to give her stunned and horrified audience are forever lost to the tides of time, but Reagan's assuring and comforting speech to the nation that night will never be.

It was while sitting at Reagan's knee, figuratively speaking, that he taught me the rudiments of conservatism—limited government, less taxes and regulations, the free market, and the emphasis on individual liberty. It wasn't until two decades later that these tenants became more than mere slogans to me, and I discovered to my chagrin that, though it may speak the language of conservatism, the Republican Party hardly governed conservatively.

The Reagan Administration also saw the rise of the Moral Majority as a major political force in national politics. This foray into the political arena came decades after the war had already been lost as Christians, and conservatives in general, retreated from the battlegrounds of public education, academia, law, entertainment, and the news media. It was a rearguard action meant to regain politically what it had already lost culturally. Whatever temporary gains it made were to be lost in the decades to come as the country rapidly grew more secular and, not coincidentally, socialist.

The policies of the Reagan Administration led to the collapse of the Soviet Union, that "evil empire" as Reagan famously called it, during the presidency of George H.W. Bush. Ironically, at the same time that socialism was experiencing its greatest defeat, its seeds planted long ago in America under the rubric of "progressivism," "liberalism," and the New Deal soon brought it to ascendancy in its greatest foe.

We realized much too late that we had, in fact, become the very enemy we had fought against during the Cold War. We desired central planning just as much as the Communists did, but we were content (for the time being) to keep businesses and property in private hands rather than bring them under pubic ownership. Both Americans and Soviets believed that they were entitled to government-provided goodies, but we were content (for the present) to hide the confiscation necessary to pay for them while the Soviets exercised their theft openly.

The only difference between America and the Soviets was the degree and means employed, not the principles espoused. The basic philosophical assumptions of egalitarianism, collectivism, and statism were shared by both the socialists in the Soviet Union and those in the socialist democracies of the West, including the United States. Though the USSR claimed to be a republic, its socialism was imposed dictatorially. In contrast, however, America imposed it democratically by an electorate who wanted it and, in fact, craved it.

We no longer desired freedom from government, but demanded certain entitlements from it. Our conception of rights became perverted, shifting from God-given natural rights that government cannot interfere with to man-made claims on what government ought to do on our behalf. As the nation would tragically learn in the decades to come, liberty and socialism are mutually exclusive and cannot coexist together. Either a nation becomes all one, or all the other.

There are only two events I can personally remember from the elder Bush's single term as president—his broken promise of no new taxes and the Gulf War. Like children throughout the ages who were fortunate enough to live far removed from the field of battle, war was something exciting and patriotic. I eagerly watched the news accounts from the front, and my friends and I busied ourselves collecting Desert Storm trading cards that featured troops and weapons used in the war. I still have them in a box in the basement, though I greatly doubt their value as anything other than mementos.

While Bush was popular with us for his leadership during the Gulf War, his image became tarnished when he broke his "read my lips" vow not to raise taxes. As a kid who wasn't going to pay any taxes for several years, Bush's betrayal had no real significance to me except that it didn't sound either conservative or consistent. But as with far too many Republicans in that era, we were too eager to turn a blind eye to the lack of conservatism practiced by our elected leaders. The goal was simply to elect Republicans; how they actually governed once in office was largely ignored.

Having spent the better part of my childhood with a Republican in the a White House, it was a rude awaking when the voters elected Bill Clinton in 1992. Having grown up in a Christian conservative community, my friends and I were shocked that the country would elect a liberal, pot-smoking womanizer as their president. It was our first realization that perhaps the rest of the country did not share our values and morals.

Other than Hillary's ever changing hairdos, the only things I personally remember about the Clinton Administration are the philandering and the 1994 mid-term electoral victory by Republicans. Far too many people accepted Clinton's lack of marital faithfulness on the ridiculous grounds that it had no effect on his job performance.

They carelessly (or intentionally) overlooked the simple fact that every adulterer runs the risk of being subjected to blackmail. More importantly, however, they failed to recognize that if his own wife can't trust him, why should the electorate? A man who can, without conscience, live a life of lies to his family can easily do so to his country. Most Americans, in fact, understood this, but refused to judge Clinton for his sexual immorality less they be judged for their own.

The 1994 mid-term elections showed that, for a time, conservatism wasn't dead after all. There were still enough voters in enough districts to send enough Republicans to Congress to stop Clinton from completely implementing his agenda. At the same time, however, there weren't enough Republicans to implement a conservative agenda (assuming they would actually do so if they could). Republicans stopped educating the electorate about conservatism, and instead nominated the moderate Bob Dole as their standard bearer in the 1996 presidential contest. As always happens with non-conservative Republican nominees, he lost.

I must close for now. Life as a prisoner of war continues its monotonous pace. Though the days and nights often blend together into one boring sameness, it is much preferable to the pain and torture that marks the experiences of so many POWs. The most interest our captors have shown in us was the execution of one of my men who tried to escape.

Even under the best of circumstances, Todd Turner, while a capable cook, was always in a nervous, fragile state of mind. But he finally broke in confinement and tried to make a break for the prison walls while they hosed us down outside in the prison yard. They shot him in the leg before he had even gone ten feet, then forced us to watch as they turned their hungry hounds on him.

Todd faced the fight with manly courage, but the ensuing bloodbath was grotesquely horrific. One of the dogs never made it back, but neither did Todd. They refused to allow us to bury him, choosing instead to leave his body as a stark reminder to would-be imitators of the fate that awaited them. My men, however, are slow learners, and such teaching techniques only makes them more hard-headed. There may be more viable avenues of escape than Todd's mad dash for the wall...

No prisoners have yet to be exchanged, though rumors continue to swirl that the Mexicans have several generals they would like to get back. In the meantime, we continue to keep hope alive in Cell No. 73 that we will be home soon, either through a prisoner exchange or by other means.

Until I can see you again, however, please know that I pray for you continually. With much love.

Your affectionate grandfather,
Col. Peter Iossi

LETTER IV

MY DEAREST GRANDCHILDREN,

Today is the Fourth of July! At least, we believe so. In a place devoid of natural light, clocks, or calendars, it is impossible to know for sure. But our surreptitious, clandestine smugglers have confirmed that today is in fact Independence Day, so we are planning on celebrating with a rousing rendition of the Star Spangled Banner during our one-hour excursion to the exercise room.

Several weeks ago the Mexicans celebrated Cinco de Mayo by bringing all of the Hispanic-Americans among my men to the exercise room to forcibly participate in the singing of the Mexican national anthem. They were lined up in rows and told, upon pain of death, to sing as loud as they could with their hands over their hearts.

My men complied, but the only song that emanated from their vocal cords was the Star Spangled Banner...in English. (Since the war begun, my men refused to speak Spanish even though most, regardless of ethnicity, could speak it fluently.) The Mexicans were infuriated and quickly silenced my men by putting a bullet in the head of my close friend Major Juan Estrada. It was his dear wife and five beautiful children that had cared for my dog Lucky before you (temporarily) adopted him.

The Mexicans once again gave my men the command to sing, and once again their singing of the Star Spangled Banner was silenced when another of their comrades fell to the ground dead. This tragic point and counterpoint of cruelty and bravery played itself out until an entire row of our men lay dead on the exercise room floor. Finally, tiring of death, the Mexicans simply decided that the remaining Hispanic-Americans had no more use for their tongues and promptly cut them out.

So today we are fighting back, if only with our voices rather than our fists. Though the Hispanic-Americans among us can no longer sing, their proud insubordination testifies to their patriotic courage more loudly than any chorus ever could. Our show of defiance may cost us our tongues or even our lives, but this is what being a self-respecting American requires. A free man does not cower in the face of fear.

Our country now has two Independence Days—the day we declared independence from Britain and the day we declared independence from the United States of America. Both days should be celebrated, for both are equally important. They are a memorial to the fact that even a people as free as Americans were can be convinced to trade away their liberty for the illusionary security of a government handout.

Once the trade is made, the promised security quickly gives way to slavery and dependency. The recipients' state of bondage may be veiled for a time under the guise of compassionate big government, but it is just as real as any found on Southern plantations of old. Like Esau, the American people sold their birthright for a bowl of stew.

If you are like most Americans, you probably have never actually read the Declaration of Independence. Please, do not delay in rectifying that dereliction of every citizen's duty to read his country's (original) birth certificate. If you should only read one book in your life, meditate on the Bible. But if you would, become a master of at least one other document—

the Declaration.

No other writing in human history so succinctly sums up the relationship between man and government:

> We hold these truths to be self-evident, that all men are created equal, that they are endowed by their Creator with certain unalienable rights, that among these are life, liberty and the pursuit of happiness [i.e., property].
>
> That to secure these rights, governments are instituted among men, deriving their just powers from the consent of the governed. That whenever any form of government becomes destructive to these ends, it is the right of the people to alter or abolish it, and to institute new government...

Like I did long ago, memorize those words, for they are the scales by which the legitimacy of government coercion is judged. The sole end of government is to secure man's unalienable right to life, liberty, and property. As the welfare state amply demonstrates, the use of coercion to serve other ends can only occur by violating these natural rights.

I have been fascinated with American history ever

since I was a child. I would read books on the American Revolution and our early presidents, and excelled in my history and civics classes at school. Thus when it came time to pick a career, I sought one that would allow me to engage with the America of our Founding Fathers that I was, and remain, in love with.

So I decided to major in political science with the goal of attending law school to study constitutional law. Despite achieving a Bachelor of Arts degree in political science, I did not graduate from college with a well-developed political philosophy. That wasn't to grow into full bloom until ten years later during the Obama presidency. For the time being, I was simply content with the rubric of conservatism I learned as a child—higher taxes bad, less government good, socialism bad, national defense good.

But while my political philosophy remained in an embarrassing state of infancy, my constitutional jurisprudence took on shape and form during my college and especially law school years. Its development had nothing to do with the tutelage of my professors, most, if not all, of whom were incorrigibly liberal, but with the influence of one book—Judge Robert Bork's Tempting of America: The Political Seduction of the Law.

His book impressed upon me the importance of the law as an immovable force that restrained politicians, judges, and citizens alike. It is not an embodiment of one's personal preferences, but a duly enacted statute passed by the representatives of the people that can only be changed in the same way it was created. Judge Bork used a scene from the play A Man for All Seasons about the life and martyrdom of Sir Thomas More to illustrate his point.

One day More's son-in-law, William Roper, asked him if he would give the Devil the benefit of the law. More, as Chancellor of England, emphatically responded in the affirmative and asked Roper if he would cut a road through the law to seize the Devil. When Roper eagerly responded that he would cut down every law in order to arrest the Devil, More cautioned him that, "when the last law was down, and the Devil turned 'round on you, where would you hide, Roper, the laws all being flat?" "Yes," More concluded, "I'd give the Devil the benefit of law, for my own safety's sake!"

I have never actually seen or read the entire play, but that scene is imprinted on my mind's stage as an illustration of the sacredness of the law. But what does the law mean, and how are we to interpret it? Words have different meanings depending on context, and the role of the judge is to determine the meaning of the language used in a statute, regulation, prior court decision, or constitutional provision and apply that meaning to a particular case.

This job is particularly important when a judge is determining the meaning of the Constitution because it is the manifestation of the fundamental will of the people. If we apply our own meaning to that document, rather than that of those who drafted and ratified it, then we have changed what they said. But the Constitution is the supreme law of the land, and neither its text nor its meaning can be changed by any other means than the laborious amendment process.

It is imperative, therefore, that the Constitution be read by judges according to the original public understanding of its words and phrases. To apply any other meaning would be to substitute the judges' will in place of the supreme and fundamental will of the people who ratified that document.

Once I understood this and sought to understand the Constitution as those who ratified it understood it, I soon realized that the country I lived in did not resemble the one created by that sacred charter. We still had the form of government envisioned by the

Founding Generation, but the substance was utterly alien to their intentions. If those who ratified the Constitution understood that it would have been exploited to create the federal government of the 20th and 21st centuries, they would have overwhelming defeated it. The America I found myself in had become a post-constitutional Leviathan.

The government born of that Constitution was intended to be one of limited, enumerated powers, almost none of which concerned domestic policies. Having just fought a revolutionary war, the Founding Generation understood that centralized power posed the greatest threat to freedom and individual rights. They knew from personal experience that politicians were addicts to power, incapable of self-control. As Thomas Jefferson foresaw, when all government power became centered in Washington, the federal government became as oppressive as Great Britain had been.

The Constitution was only passed because its supporters assured the public that the new federal government lacked the power to threaten their rights. Writing in the Federalist Papers, Alexander Hamilton argued that a Bill of Rights was unnecessary because the new government would lack the authority, for instance, to infringe on a person's speech or free exercise of religion.

The federal government was never designed for 435 Congressmen and 100 Senators to wield authority over every area of life for 320 million people. It was no wonder, then, that Americans began to feel that they had no voice in government. Washington unconstitutionally mandates one-size-fits-all policies on local issues that should have been left to more responsive local representatives. And if we didn't care for our local policies, at least we could always vote with our feet by moving elsewhere.

In order to preserve our liberties, the Founding Generation created a federal government with only the following fourteen powers:

1. Borrow money.
2. Regulate foreign trade and create an interstate free trade zone.
3. Regulate naturalization.
4. Create national bankruptcy laws.
5. Regulate currency and punish counterfeiting.
6. Established the post office and post roads.
7. Create copyright and patent laws.
8. Provide for the federal judiciary.
9. Prosecute piracies.
10. Declare war and provide for a military.

11.Govern federal lands and admit new states.

12.Regulate the time, place, and manner of casting federal ballots.

13.Regulate interstate comity laws.

14.Collect and spend taxes for the above.

That's it, only fourteen specific grants of power. None of which involved health care, education, student loans, Medicare, drought relief, Social Security, or growing the economy. Those areas, and all others not enumerated above, were to be regulated, if at all, by state legislators. The Constitution was to be an equal opportunity denial of federal authority. In the America I found myself in, however, the Bill of Rights had, ironically, become the only colorable restraints on federal power. Federalism was dead.

I must get this letter "in the mail" before our Fourth of July fireworks—figuratively, we hope—later today. With much love and prayers until I can write (or see you) again.

Your affectionate grandfather,
Col. Peter Iossi

LETTER V

MY DEAREST GRANDCHILDREN,

Please rest assured that there were no literal Fourth of July fireworks as a consequence of our defiant singing of the Star Spangled Banner. Our guards were not outraged that non-Hispanic Americans would sing the American national anthem, and the Hispanic-Americans among us were unable to vocalize their patriotism due to our captives' earlier display of cruelty.

But while they were not outraged to the level of physical violence, the Mexicans could not let such insolence go entirely unpunished. So instead of serving us rats dressed up as Tex-Mex, they decided to just serve us rats—of the raw, squiggly, and very much alive variety—and only rats for food. At every meal time the food slots would open and, instead of a tray filled with our normal fare, two live rats for each inmate were dropped into our cells.

The first several times caught us off guard and left us scrambling to catch and kill the little vermin. Fortunately we didn't have many belongings, leaving them with few places to hide. By the second day we learned to wait by the food slot when we heard the dinner car rolling in the hallway in order to catch the rodents with our shirts.

We refused to eat them, opting instead to flush them down the toilet after beating their heads against the cell walls. The forced diet of rats came to a thankful end after ten days, and I eagerly embraced the return of our normal prison rations. We may still be served rats, but at least they are of the dead and cooked variety.

Ironically, we may have engaged in our musical protest with the wrong national anthem. The last I was aware, our new country had yet to decide on a national anthem, though the Star Spangled Banner was regularly played among our men. But I doubt the United States will cede her national anthem to us, which will leave us to find another melody to adopt.

Secession in which both sides lay claim to the nation's historic identity is rare in the world as most such movements take place along ethnic, nationalistic fault lines in which neither side wants anything to do with the other. But the fall of America is different, with each faction believing that they are the rightful heirs to the national anthem, flag, motto, bird, and monuments as emblems of her legacy.

Please do not let our new country, as Benjamin Franklin once suggested, make the turkey the national bird. Being a native Iowan, perhaps a Hawkeye would be a suitable substitute. They should keep the flag elegantly simple and, as always, red, white, and blue. Whatever our new national motto is, it should be practiced and not just proclaimed.

If we must choose a new national anthem, perhaps My Country 'Tis of Thee would be appropriate. We used to begin every morning in elementary school by reciting it, and I loved its first and fourth stanzas:

My country, 'tis of thee,
Sweet land of liberty,
Of thee I sing;
Land where my fathers died,
Land of the pilgrims' pride,
From ev'ry mountainside
Let freedom ring!

Our fathers' God to Thee,

Author of liberty,

To Thee we sing.

Long may our land be bright,

With freedom's holy light,

Protect us by Thy might,

Great God our King.

Of course, we didn't recite the fourth stanza in public school because it contained too many references to God in it. That would have violated the wall of separation of church and state that judges, replacing the original public understanding of the Constitution with their own prejudices, had reinterpreted the First Amendment to require.

But it was somehow constitutional for the federal government to spend billions of dollars on public education, with as many strings attached as they desired, despite the lack of constitutional authority to do so. Congress has only the power to tax and spend in furtherance of one of its enumerated powers described in my last letter, none of which include education. As history has amply demonstrated, if Congress can regulate at will through its taxing authority, than it can no longer be described as a government of limited, enumerated powers.

Sadly, the president who enacted the most extensive federal involvement in education was a Republican and my first commander-in-chief—George W. Bush. While I personally liked him, in spite of the media's biased and unfair caricature of him, conservatism in general and a belief in federalism in particular were not his strong suit.

Compassionate conservatism. It is easy to mock the term now, decades later, but while still in my political infancy I thought it an apt slogan to show the world that conservatives had bleeding hearts just like liberals. We weren't angry, white, rich old men or, even if we were, at least we had hearts of gold. After all, all that matters in politics is good intentions...with other people's money.

Though I suspected it at the time, it wasn't until much later that I realized that "compassionate conservatism" was just big government socialism sugar-coated as conservatism. George W. Bush understood that he could only win if he appealed to the masses as a political Santa Claus, but that he needed to dress it up in conservative terms so his base wouldn't desert him.

While my political awakening lay years in the future, I knew that Bush's legislative agenda that included No Child Left Behind and Medicare prescription drug reform lacked any constitutional authority. But at the time I was still in law school and, since no one else seemed to share my convictions, decided it was futile to make a fuss over such technicalities as the Constitution. It wasn't until the rise of the Tea Party a decade latter that I realized I wasn't nearly as alone as I thought I was.

Like most Americans who lived through that day, I vividly remember that Tuesday morning on September 11, 2001 when 19 Islamic terrorists hijacked four planes, three of them finding their intended targets. The feelings of horror, confusion, patriotism, and revenge pulsed in the heart of every American that day, and for several weeks thereafter. Human nature being what it is, however, those feelings for most Americans slowly died a quiet death amongst the pleasures and toils of daily living, arising to barely a whimper of outcry when Islamic terrorists marked the 11th anniversary of 9/11 by killing a U.S. ambassador and three other Americans in Benghazi.

For me, however, and for a number of other Americans, the passion never died. As in the Cold War of my youth, America now had another mortal enemy and his name was Islamic terrorism. Ironically, while America had to face and win this new war, the old enemy of socialism was quietly but steadily gaining converts and victories back on the home front. But because it peacefully took over buildings one convert at a time rather than blow them up, its rise escaped the notice of most Americans.

I wrestled with my conscience in the months after 9/11, desiring to join the military out of patriotic duty, but committed to finishing the last year and a half of law school. The deciding question was how I could best defend my country. I saw a clear and attainable path to victory against Islamic terrorists, but I saw no such path to victory for constitutionalism in my country's courtrooms.

While my choice seemed clear, it was complicated by the birth of your father the previous Christmas Day. Though your grandmother and I had married the March before law school, we had planned on waiting to have kids until after I had graduated. God apparently had other plans, as Jonathan came along nine months after the honeymoon.

Wars, however, are not fought only by childless men, but by countless men and women serving in harm's way thousands of miles from their young families. Therefore, after much prayer and thought, your grandmother and I decided that I was being called to the military, child or no child.

So at Christmas I announced to my shocked family that I had joined the Marine Corp and would be starting basic training soon. Though caught off guard, my family was enthusiastically supportive of my decision, save for my mother. I know of no mother who is happy with her child's decision to join the military. Extremely proud, yes; happy, no.

I intentionally eschewed a career as a military lawyer and the dull life of pouring over procurement contracts, employment regulations, wills of those about to be shipped off to the front, etc. I didn't want to sit on the sidelines of the war or, worse yet, micromanage it by second-guessing the legalities of decisions made by those on the ground. Instead, despite the perils, I desired the honor and responsibility of leading men into battle.

After extensive training, I was finally commissioned as a second lieutenant and served in the 1st Marine Division during the invasion of Iraq in 2003. Though a soldier's duty is to follow, not question, his orders, I was not an enthusiastic supporter of the war. I did not believe that Saddam poised a direct threat, nor did it seem likely that he would be foolish enough to give a weapon of mass destruction to terrorist groups. Also, being no fan of the UN, I found it repulsive that we were, in part, going to war to enforce a UN sanction.

It was my hope, however, that we could establish a new Iraqi government that would be a US ally and a buffer between Iran's ambitions and the rest of the Middle East. In retrospect, that was a laughably silly notion. Even assuming it justified war, a dubious proposition, America never had the stomach for nation building, and Iraq soon became Iran's client state. There had been no love lost between Iraqis and Iranians under Saddam, but by the time we left it was a lovefest.

Tiring of nation building after two deployments in Iraq, I joined the Marine Special Forces and, after yet more training, found myself deployed to Afghanistan just as the US economy started to sink in 2008. Though still involved in nation building, at least I had plenty of opportunities to kill the allies and enablers of the perpetrators of 9/11.

Back home, however, America was suffering from the Great Recession. Even though my political awakening was still a few years away, I remember cringing as the Bush Administration bailed out private companies and sought to stimulate the economy. Government intervention in the market place in order to "save" capitalism didn't sound very conservative to me.

For if one believes that the free market cannot save itself, it logically leads to the Marxist conclusion that perhaps it shouldn't be free at all. After all, if government knows best how to revive the economy, than some degree of government command and control becomes necessary not only to prevent recessions in the future, but to grow the economy at a faster rate than it can do itself. Unfortunately, I was politically naive enough not to realize just how much government command and control of our mixed economy already existed, and that Bush's policies were simply a logical extension of government behavior of the past century.

I must close for now. With much love and prayers until I can write (or see you) again.

Your affectionate grandfather,
Col. Peter Iossi

LETTER VI

MY DEAREST GRANDCHILDREN,

My old Marine base during many of my years in the Corps has fallen to the Mexicans. Word has reached me that Camp Pendleton was finally captured two weeks ago, along with the greater San Diego metropolitan area. I am surprised, but extremely proud, that they were able to hold out as long as they did against overwhelming forces.

Now all that remains of the short-lived Republic of California is the Central Valley of California, the Sierra Nevada, northern Nevada, and a stump of Utah. With the defeat of the Marines at Camp Pendleton, however, there is precious little to stop the Mexican advance on those remaining territories.

Mexico might be content to stop after capturing

the remaining lands of the Republic, but the city of Los Angeles and the rest of the newly–formed Pacific States of America shouldn't count on it. Unfortunately, the citizens of LA, Sacramento, San Francisco, Portland, Seattle, and Boise aren't known for being a fearsome, jingoistic people. Maybe they could keep the Mexicans at bay with tributes of Starbucks and tenured professorships in women's studies.

Fortunately, our armies in Texas are still holding their ground, but victory, for either side, is far from certain. It has become an ugly and costly war of attrition along a vast frontline. There is talk that both sides may agree to an armistice dividing Texas in two, but that likely will not occur until the ground turns red with blood.

It is absolutely essential to the future of our new country that we hold the major population centers and the Gulf Coast of Texas. Our national morale and economy would take an enormous hit without the colossus that is Texas. While Kansas City may be our capital, Texas is the economic and political engine of our country. Without her, we would be largely rudderless, having no other state that carries half the weight that she does. Mexico can have the dessert, but we must be able to keep the eastern half of Texas.

Keeping Mexico at bay is also vital to our long-term national interests, for if Mexico would add Texas to its conquests of Arizona, Colorado, New Mexico, Utah, Nevada, and Southern California, she would easily become the most powerful, and consequently most dangerous, country in North America. She knows this, which is why she will not give up the fight for Texas until she is bled dry. We must, therefore, make her bleed.

As we fight militarily to secure our country's future, we must not neglect the fight on the home front to create the societal mores and constitutional provisions necessary to ensure that our hard-won liberties are not lost. For if we win the battle of bullets but lose the one for the hearts and souls of our new country, our victory is but an illusion. We will soon become the Leviathan we are seceding from.

It wasn't until President Obama was elected in 2008 that my political philosophy matured beyond mere conservative campaign slogans. The only good thing I can say about Obama is that he wasn't the worst president America ever had; that was yet to come. But it was under Obama that the seeds of socialism sown a century ago would finally reach political ascendancy.

It wasn't so much Obama's policies that led to my conversion to real, principled conservatism, but the hypocritical response by the elected Republicans. In criticizing Obama while simultaneously pursuing the same policies, I realized that far too many elected Republicans offered no real alternative to the statism of Big Government. Though they cloaked their policies in the mantra of conservatism, the Republican establishment had simply become socialism–lite.

Repulsed by the behavior of Republicans, I sought to develop a principled, consistent political philosophy. The key, I realized, was the quote from the Declaration of Independence I mentioned in an earlier letter:

> We hold these truths to be self–evident, that all men are created equal, that they are endowed by their Creator with certain unalienable rights, that among these are life, liberty and the pursuit of happiness [i.e., property].
>
> That to secure these rights, governments are instituted among men, deriving their just powers from the consent of the governed. That whenever any form

of government becomes destructive to these ends, it is the right of the people to alter or abolish it, and to institute new government...

Man is created free and equal in the image of God and is bestowed by his Creator with unalienable and innate rights to life, free agency (liberty), and the fruit of his labor (property). The "Laws of Nature and of Nature's God" dictate that no one has the right to interfere with another's natural rights.

Because man is fallen, however, and prone to violate this natural law, government was established to restrain this evil. Men delegated their natural right of self-defense to the government to serve as an impartial arbitrator of their rights. The law is simply a substitution of common force for individual force, and can therefore do only what an individual has the natural and lawful right to do—protect persons, liberties, and properties, and to maintain the right of each.

Unfortunately, government, because it consists of fallen, sinful men, will abuse and corrupt the power entrusted to them. While a necessary evil, government upholds the natural law without offending it by preserving it from foreign and domestic threats (i.e., national defense and a criminal and civil justice system). It also has a role in providing for those limited cases that the free market is unable to provide for (e.g., infrastructure and public utilities).

However, when government moves from being an impartial arbitrator of natural rights to regulating man's enjoyment of them, it must satisfy the presumption of liberty— the most local form of democratic government feasible that addresses a necessary public interest by using the least restrictive means available which do not deprive one of his rights in order to give them to another (i.e., redistribution of wealth or forced equality of outcomes).

It is not enough to live under a democratic form of government. Hitler was democratically elected, and then democratically given dictatorial powers. The terrorist group Hamas was democratically elected in the Gaza Strip, as was the Muslim Brotherhood in Egypt. In the years to come, our own president became little better than an elected monarch.

A democracy, therefore, is not an end but a means by which to diffuse power and hold it accountable so as to check its abuses. Government is the business of exercising coercion and control, and it becomes no more legitimate simply because its form is democratic rather than totalitarian. Such power is only legitimate when used to protect man's natural and unalienable rights to life, liberty, and property.

Tragically, there were precious few politicians who talked about liberty anymore in America. Instead of worshipping individual freedom, the religion in the birthplace of modern democracy was the god of statism. Rather than relying on Providence, man turned to the state for his daily bread. The only sacrifice required was national suicide—the exchange of rights for handouts, liberty for domestication, responsibility for nannyism.

This new god, however, was not a franchise of any particular political party. Both Republicans and Democrats worshipped at the altar of the state, believing in its saving power for mankind. Political elections became a religious festival of state worship in which competing political saviors offered us earthly salvation in return for genuflection.

It became abundantly clear to me that as long as conservatism merely played lip service to its principles rather than actually apply them, it could never serve as an effective alternative to statism. So long as it remained an ad hoc, knee-jerk reaction to the socialist welfare state, it moved from principled opposition to big government to a slow, hypocritical accommodation to it.

Absent principles, a conservative simply became a lukewarm statist who promised the same mana from government, but without the righteous zeal of a true believer. Conservatism could only become a viable alternative to statism if it renounced this idolatry in all its forms and remembered, with Lord Acton, that all power corrupts and must therefore be denied rather than desired.

Only a principled conservatism that pledged to protect man's God-given unalienable rights rather than sacrifice them could serve as an effective check on statism. Because nearly every act of the modern Leviathan is an infringement on man's rights, the conservative response is "no, you can't" unless and until the legislation satisfies the presumption of liberty.

My political awakening, long overdue, had finally arrived, just in time for the rise of the Tea Party and the conservative tidal wave in the 2010 mid-term elections. It would, alas, prove to be liberty's last gasp of air.

I must get this in the mail before the "postman" leaves. With much love and prayers until I can write (or see you) again.

Your affectionate grandfather,
Col. Peter Iossi

LETTER VII

MY DEAREST GRANDCHILDREN,

One of the overriding concerns in the 2010 mid-term elections was our mounting national debt. Largely absent from our political discourse for over a decade, Republicans were, for the time being, eager to tell voters that they were serious about curbing our nation's unsustainable spending.

The fundamental driver of our debt, however, was our greed, and Republicans had no intention of curbing the public's love of other people's money. But without such abstention, our addiction to selfishness continued to push our debt to levels never before reached by any nation in history. Our national soul was bankrupted long before we were.

Both major political parties in America found

themselves unwilling to just say "no" to their constituents. Instead, they increasingly won reelection by bribing the voters with all kinds of goodies provided by the government. Political elections became a contest between competing Santa Clauses, except that politicians, unlike St. Nick, only gave away other people's toys.

During the campaign season we would all get in line to sit on Santa's lap at rallies and town hall events, hoping for a chance to give him our wish lists. And all the would-be Santas would assure us that only they, and not the other guy, have the magical touch to deliver our presents to us on Christmas Eve.

While it's easy to blame the politicians for this folly, it only worked because the American people gave full vent to their greed. In a democracy we get the political system we vote for, and what the American people wanted was an ever increasing redistributionist welfare state that gave them their "fair share."

At the time, most Americans still publicly denounced the idea of wealth redistribution, except when it came to their own sense of entitlement. Most decried those who lived off the labor of other people, except when it came to their own government provided jobs and benefits. As the Nobel-winning economist Milton Friedman once sarcastically put it, "Of course none of us are greedy. It's only the other fellow who's greedy."

The federal government was never able to reduce its spending once the electorate figured out that they could vote themselves other people's money. While many throughout the years denounced greed on Wall Street as something evil, few had the courage to denounce the greed of the electorate as their addiction to the public treasury continued without pause.

Everyone is greedy, the only difference is how they seek to satisfy their greed. In the free market, the capitalist seeks to satisfy his greed only by offering innovative goods and services consumers demand at a price they want. His greed can only be satisfied when the buyer's greed is also voluntarily satisfied.

In a welfare state, however, where everyone is living off the trough of big government, people seek to satisfy their greed through coercion. It is simply legalized plunder operated by robbers armed with the threat of government force and imprisonment. It is wholly incompatible with government's sole responsibility to protect man's natural and unalienable rights to the fruit of his own labor.

In order to ensure man's right to property, the Fifth Amendment provided that property could only be seized by the government for a public use if just compensation was paid to the land owner. In Kelo v. New London, the Supreme Court eviscerated the term "public use" when it held that the government could take property from A to give to B in the name of economic rejuvenation.

Public outrage was immediate and hypocritical. For while new legislation was passed in numerous states prohibiting taking real property from A to give to B, nothing was done to prevent the same thing from occurring with income property. It was a distinction without a difference.

For if government cannot take some of your physical property to, say, give to an ethanol plant in the name of economic rejuvenation, why is it morally permissible for it to do so through the tax code? If the government cannot seize the food in your refrigerator to feed the hungry to create a better able-bodied workforce, why can it seize a portion of your income to do the same?

If it cannot pillage the medicine in your cabinet to prevent people from dying each year without health insurance, why can it accomplish the same thing through raiding your checkbook? The only distinction is one of evasiveness and degree, not one of principle. Perhaps this coerciveness might have been felt more poignantly if taxpayers had to actually write Uncle Sam a check every April 15th rather than have their taxes automatically withheld by their employer.

The principles of the Fifth Amendment's eminent domain protections should have applied with equal moral force to the government's taxing power. Taxation should only be limited to providing revenue for government's three core public responsibilities— national defense, a criminal and civil justice system, and those functions, such as infrastructure and public utilities, that the free market is unable to perform. Wealth redistribution, in contrast, has no public function; it merely gives from one individual to another for his own personal use.

Tragically, there were too few politicians who either believed this or were willing to make the argument to the public. Instead, Republicans embraced the entitlement state, running on promises to save such wealth redistributionist programs as Social Security and Medicare.

Republicans, no less than Democrats, were also eager to manipulate the tax code to engage in legalized plunder. They had no problem, for instance, with taxing the rich more than the middle class, it was just a question of how much more the rich should be made to pay. To borrow the overused phrase of the Obama presidency, Republicans and Democrats only differed on the "fair share" of the tax burden the rich should carry.

One of the earliest proponents of this progressive tax system was Karl Marx, who wanted the government to determine how much individual income is "enough" and to confiscate the rest in the form of taxation. This, in turn, raised the obvious question of how much individual income is "enough." The answer, invariably, is always enough to keep the gravy train from Uncle Sugar coming without raising taxes on the middle class who, not coincidentally, make up a majority of the electorate.

While no doubt appealing to the avarice of voters, the arbitrary confiscation of one's property is the denial of the individual's unalienable right to equal protection before the law. Government no longer serves as an initial arbitrator of man's rights when it discriminates against some merely because the fruit of their labor produced in the exercise of those rights exceeds those of other individuals. Only a proportional tax in which all must pay the same percentage satisfies the equal protection of the law.

But not only does a progressive tax penalize a man's unalienable right to the fruit of his labor, it takes from those with more to give to those with less, either directly in the form of government services and welfare programs or indirectly by reducing their tax burden. It is simply theft made legal by majority vote. But regardless of its philanthropic spirit, government cannot fulfill its obligation to protect one's property while simultaneously plundering it.

Unfortunately, without a political party to tell them no, the envy of the electorate continued unabated. They forgot the commandment given long ago on Mount Sinai that "thou shall not covet." Legalized robbery became institutionalized as a way of life in America. This greed became America's Achille's heel. We met the enemy, and belatedly realized that the enemy was us.

As the voter's addiction to other people's money continued to escalate uncontrollably, so did the nation's debt. While the progressive tax and welfare programs had been around for nearly a century, under President Obama the greed they represented was legitimized and exploited like never before. And, rather than posing any sort of brake on this bankruptcy of the American soul, the Republican

Party sought to save and reform it for future generations. Both parties woefully failed to understand that the only way to break an addiction is by repentance and abstinence, not encouragement and normalization.

But while all this was taking place, I was deployed a second time to Afghanistan, followed by covert missions to such hot spots as Egypt, Libya, and Syria. Our role in the "Arab Spring" was to provide money and guns to the rebels and gather intelligence. Sadly, much of the intelligence we gathered was ignored by the Obama Administration, who refused to discard the rose-colored glasses they had acquired in the ivory league indoctrination camps of liberalism.

They were unwilling to acknowledge that democracy in the Middle East simply meant replacing areligious dictators with democratically-elected dictators under Islamic law. While certainly inhumane, at least the former were realistic, practical, and open to an engagement, though at times strenuous, with the West. While just as inhumane, if not more so, the later were ruthless in their interpretation of Sharia law at both home and abroad. The West, particularly the United States, was the Great Satan that had to be resisted, defeated, and humiliated.

This point was aptly illustrated when Islamic terrorists celebrated the 11th anniversary of 9/11 by attacking the U.S. consulate in Benghazi and brutally killing our ambassador and three other Americans. Though still classified in the vaults of the Pentagon, my team and I were a scant thirty miles away that night and could have easily stopped the attack...if we had known about it.

But the command never came. My men and I were furious when we learned of the attack the following day. Furious and guilty. For though we understood that there was no way we could be responsible for the actions of others, the guilt of knowing that we could have saved our men if only we had known was overwhelming.

We vowed that day never again to stand idly by as Americans died at the hands of our enemies, even if we were given a direct order to stand down. If we were in a position to act, we would. It was a decision that would prove monumental in our lives.

Equally important was the distrust we developed for our commander-in-chief. We never really cared for him and had considered his military decisions to be too politically driven. Chief among them was his decision to order a troop surge in Afghanistan while simultaneously announcing a withdrawal date divorced of any relationship to victory on the ground. You never put the lives of American soldiers at risk simply so you can show you are doing something by "surging," while at the same time announcing the coming end of the war, regardless of whether the surge works.

But his decision the night of September 11, 2012, to do nothing while Americans died, despite ample military assets in the region, was unforgivable. Though it never came to the light of day, we learned that he was informed of the attack while it was taking place, but abrogated his responsibility to instead pack and go to bed ahead of a campaign fundraising trip to California. His administration then lied to the American people about the nature of the attack, blaming it on a movie that no one ever saw rather than acknowledging that it was planned and executed by terrorists.

I never again trusted the motives of my commander-in-chiefs. Say what you will about President George W. Bush, at least you knew he treated the men and women of the armed forces with tremendous respect and dignity. Since 9/11/12, however, I never again trusted a commander-in-chief to do anything other than sacrifice those under him, including soldiers, to advance his own agenda. Cynical, perhaps, but realistic. In America's secular, post–constitutional, socialist democracy, Caesar lived only for Caesar.

I must close for now. I miss you terribly, and long for us to be together again soon. With much love and prayers until I can write (or see you) again.

Your affectionate grandfather,

Col. Peter Iossi

LETTER VIII

MY DEAREST GRANDCHILDREN,

Yesterday was September 16, the day on which Mexico celebrates its independence from Spain two-hundred years ago. While usually peaceful, here in prison the ceremonies took on a macabre nature as the guards commemorated the anniversary with bloodshed.

Considering the Hispanic-Americans among my men as traitors to Mexican nationalism, our captives wished to give them one last chance to repent or face the gallows. Though staring death in the face, my men bravely refused to renounce their citizenship to our country and bend their knees to Mexico.

Incensed that every single one of them maintained their love for a country other than Mexico, the enraged guards mercilessly mowed them down where they stood. The gallows, unused, were left to cast their shadow over the prison yard as a foreboding reminder of what unpredictable turns the future may take.

The guards waited a day for the blood to dry and the bodies to stiffen and smell before they forced us to cleanse the exercise room from any sign of their cruelty the day before. The gruesome labor was slowed by the flow of our tears and our inability to control the nauseating sensations emanating from our stomachs. We were battle-hardened soldiers used to seeing death, but nothing prepared us for the senseless slaughter of our brothers in arms.

As always, the feeling of profound loss and sorrow at the killing of innocent Americans turned quickly to patriotic rage among my men. While it did not yet take the form of physical action, the desire for revenge was very real and very personal. Our hope is still for a prisoner exchange or, as increasingly seems more plausible, an escape attempt. But if we are able to kill a few of the guards as we make our exodus, so much the better.

Of course, the deaths of my men, this Second Mexican-American War, and the collapse of America were hardly imaginable during the election of 2012, though perhaps they should have been. That election was the last opportunity for the country to have a national debate over the big picture of where America was heading. The Republicans, however, nominated a flip-flopping Massachusetts liberal who was unable and unwilling to articulate a principled conservative message.

Both parties, up and down the ticket, engaged in their usual practice of bribing the voters with other people's money. They did this not only with promises of handouts from the public treasury, but with pledges to force the "free market" to provide free birth control, or affordable housing, or more jobs, or health insurance for 25-year-olds living at home or those with preexisting conditions. Whatever an important constituency desired, the "free market" would be forced to furnish.

This demand for a mixed economy in which private enterprise is under the command and control of the government is premised in socialism—the conviction that government action is needed to make the free market fairer and more equitable. It is the mistaken belief, shared by both Republicans and Democrats, that individual rights are the citizens' dutiful sacrifice on the altar of a collectivist utopian society achievable only by government planning.

Socialism in Western democracies has often been cloaked in the mantra of compassion—the desire to produce greater equalization of outcomes by protecting individuals from the vicissitudes of the free market. It is the conviction that government intervention is necessary to make the free market "work for everyone."

Regardless of the means adopted, the goal of socialism is to make such things as jobs, college education, health insurance, secure retirement, and homes more affordable and universal than they would otherwise be in the free market. It is, in short, the belief in the saving power of the government to provide the American Dream more effectively than capitalism.

The state can only achieve this mission, however, through economic manipulation that always results in the indirect subsidization of some consumers at the expense of others as a byproduct of "compassionate" regulations that "protect" an industry, shift costs of products, create union monopolies, establish wage, price, and rent controls, etc.

Far too many politicians in America showed no qualms about imposing mandates on businesses to force them into contracts that they found financially objectionable. They forgot that, in a free market, parties enter into contracts when both sides have something to gain from it. In contrast, when a contract is government mandated, one side always gains at the other's loss.

These "compassionate" government mandates always costs businesses something, and that cost is always passed on to consumers. It is, in essence, an indirect and hidden sales tax, much of it imposed by an unelected and barely accountable bureaucracy. Government can only make the "free market" fair for some at the expense of others. It is unable to perform acts of charity without robbing someone else. It cannot build some up without tearing others down.

But this is hardly consistent with government's sole responsibility to protect man's unalienable rights to life, liberty, and property. The task of government is to maintain universal justice by the equal protection of all persons, all property, all rights, all products of labor, and all interests. It is impossible for government to fulfill this mission when it attempts to make the free market more egalitarian.

There is no middle ground. The market (and thus consumers) are either free or they aren't. The choice is either the equal protection of all, or the sacrifice of some in the name of the collective good. The former is called freedom, the later is called socialism. The former believes in individual rights, the later only in the rights of the government. The former is founded on a belief in the Laws of Nature and of Nature's God, the later in which the state alone becomes the moral judge of both the means used and the ends pursued.

There is no form of government as free, democratic, and equal as the free market. It is free in that it leaves the individual free to choose from a myriad of choices without threat of coercion. It is a democracy in which each consumer has an equal voice to buy precisely what he voted for in a competitive market free from the concentration of power, whether in the hands of government, the monopolist, or labor unions. It provides equality of opportunity in an unrivaled meritocracy in which hard work, rather than political favors and crony capitalism, is rewarded.

In contrast, the sacrifice of unalienable rights demanded by American politicians is premised on the wholly unwarranted belief that government can put other people's money to better use than they can themselves. It is a fundamental distrust of the free market and the decisions people make about how to spend their own money. Unhappy with allowing individual consumers to unconsciously decide who gets what, when, and how in a competitive free market, they believe that government can do a better job managing the economy.

The reality, however, is that a command and control economy is self-defeating. The redistribution of wealth that always occurs in a mixed economy destroys economic growth, productivity, innovations, wages, and jobs. In the free market, capitalism only works when it is advantageous to both parties. Wealth is only created by cooperation, not by one at the expense of the other.

This mutual motive for profit creates the most efficient use of capital by directing it to productive businesses with improved products consumers demand at the lower prices they desire. Socialism, on the other hand, takes money out of the hands of consumers and producers where it would have been used most effectively.

This inefficiency results in a net loss to the country. By redirecting capital from the efficient to subsidize the inefficient, total productivity and, consequently, wages and jobs are reduced. In effect, the pie gets smaller, not larger; the economy slows rather than grows. Even minimal socialist intervention, therefore, creates far more poverty than it can ever hope to alleviate. In contrast, however, the free market is the greatest poverty program the world has ever known.

Tragically, Americans long ago lost sight of the fundamental principle that government cannot create wealth, it can only transfer it from the productive to the unproductive. It cannot create jobs, it can only transfer them from efficient businesses to inefficient ones. It does not invest in the free market, it only picks winners at the expense of losers.

In short, a compassionate government is to be despised and abhorred, for its compassion is always accompanied by a ball and chains. Government coerced compassion is nothing less than slavery for both the subsidizer and the subsidized. The former works to provide for the later, while the later becomes dependent on the former's involuntary servitude. It is a cruel, dehumanizing farce that bankrupts the national soul.

I hope to write (or see you) again soon, but until then know that you are loved and that I never cease praying for you.

Your affectionate grandfather,
Col. Peter Iossi

LETTER IX

MY DEAREST GRANDCHILDREN,

I cried upon Obama's reelection in 2012, not because it would mean another four years of Obama, but because of what it said about the state of the American electorate. They rejected a candidate with even the mildest application of conservatism and elected to stick with Obama even after the disaster that was his first term.

It became clear that the American people had openly embraced Big Government and truly desired the socialist democracies that bankrupted Europe. The seeds of socialism that had been planted a century ago had finally blossomed into fruition. After generations of deluding themselves that they were different from their European cousins, Americans finally came out of the closet in 2012 and reelected the most socialist president, up to that point, in American history.

In a country in which socialism was firmly entrenched as the predominate political philosophy, conservatism would never again win a national election. It is impossible for a party of personal responsibility and freedom to survive in a country that demands salvation by Big Government. The American people no longer wanted liberty; they openly demanded Santa Claus.

The Republican Party was finished as a viable national party. For the first time, Republicans realized after the 2012 election that they were no longer living in a center-right country. They now understood that the American people were willing to voluntarily subject themselves to a Matrix in return for empty promises of freedom from care, worry, fear, responsibility, or sense of mortality. The lure of security was more important to Americans than the liberties they claimed to prize.

The party establishment, who cared more about winning elections than principles, decided the GOP must evolve to survive. The Party, shedding even a pretense of being conservative, sought to increase government and give out presents with as much vigor as the Democrats. Socialism became the only major political party in America, it just had a liberal wing that went by the name Democrat and a conservative wing named Republican.

In disgust, I switched my registration to Independent, only registering as a Republican to vote in the primaries (which became less and less worth the effort to do). I was hardly alone, as droves of social, economic, and libertarian conservatives left the Republican Party, never to return. A shrunken party, already struggling with an image imposed on it by the mainstream media, was never able to regain the White House. In the future it would hold either the House or the Senate, but never both at the same time.

By the time the mask was torn off America's ardent love-affair with socialism in the 2012 election, the bill was coming due for their secret dalliance of the last century and its payment would bankrupt the nation. The political talk after the 2012 election was about the looming "fiscal cliff" at the end of the year brought about by scheduled tax hikes and spending cuts.

The sad reality, however, is that we were already over the edge of the real fiscal cliff and were free-falling towards the bottom. We were just experiencing the pillaging before the eventual thud at the end. The single biggest threat America faced was its pending, inevitable default on its promises, but no one in Washington had the political courage to point it out, much less do anything about it.

America's default was assured in 2012. It was only a question of when we would default, to whom, and what the consequences would be. There was only one option that would make the coming pain tolerable—switching off the gravy train from Uncle Sugar. But by 2012, no politician could have advocated that and hoped to win reelection. So no one did, and I am writing you the subsequent tale of sorrow from Cell No. 73 as a prisoner of that fate.

The debt at the beginning of Obama's second term was $16.4 trillion. While staggering and growing at a rate of a trillion dollars every nine months, it did not include the government's unfunded liabilities (i.e., the money it needed to borrow to keep all of its future entitlement promises). Estimates at the time of this future debt ranged from $60 trillion to $240 trillion. It didn't matter what the actual number was; it couldn't be paid.

Despite the unavoidable math, the American people continued to delude themselves into thinking that their debt could be paid, but that it would be the problem of future generations. Sadly, neither assumption was true—the total liabilities of the United States could never be paid back, but the default was to be felt by current generations.

While it continued to pay the interest on its debt, America in 2012 no longer made any effort to pay off its principle. Instead, it simply "rolled over" its principle by selling new bonds to pay for the old ones when they came due. Like other Ponzi schemes, it could work indefinitely until you no longer have enough new money coming in to pay the old debt.

America's creditors understood this game and continued to play it so long as they were confident that there would be buyers of new Treasury bonds so the government could in turn use that money to pay them. They knew that the United States could never pay its current and future principle, but were, for the time being, confident that they wouldn't be stuck holding the "hot potato" when time eventually ran out.

In short, the real debt fear was that lenders would no longer want to buy our bonds any more, leaving us without other people's money to pay back existing principle when the game of musical chairs ended. The day was fast approaching that, if we didn't impose a debt limit upon ourselves, the rest of the world would do it for us.

The math made that tipping point an unavoidable certainty within a few short years. Already, in 2012, the country's mandatory spending (i.e., debt interest plus entitlements such as Social Security and Medicare) hovered at or above our total tax revenue. This meant that, even if we had cut spending on everything else—defense, homeland security, prisons, infrastructure, education, etc.—we still couldn't balance the budget.

That level of unsustainability was incurable. With 10,000 seniors retiring every single day, the drivers of our debt were current entitlement spending on Social Security and Medicare. Up through the 2012 election, a few Republicans were willing to talk about reforming these entitlement programs for those 54 and younger. But as we realized too late, current entitlement spending on those 55 and older was going to bankrupt the country long before future entitlement spending would.

No politician, however, who dreamed of reelection would dare breath a word about reforming Social Security and Medicare for those currently or soon to be dependent on those programs. Roughly 50 million people were enrolled in either Social Security, Medicare, or both in 2012, a number that was soon to jump exponentially. In the "land of the free," nearly 1/6 of the population found themselves dependent on the federal government for their most basic needs.

That reality alone should have shocked Americans into rejecting socialism, but it failed to even raise an eyebrow. When politicians first promised Americans to look after their money and save for their retirement better than they could themselves, they should have been driven from office in fear and shame. Instead, 150 years after Americans threw off the shackles of British tyranny, they gladly turned over their life savings to Big Government and thereby ensured their serfdom.

Americans preferred to think that they had earned their Social Security and Medicare benefits by paying into those programs during their working years. If true, however, these entitlement programs would not be a drain on the public treasury at all. Instead, the money people had paid into locked retirement boxes would be theirs to use during their sunset years.

The laughable absurdity of the claim that these benefits were earned is all too easily apparent now, but far too many people believed it then. These entitlement programs were Ponzi schemes in which the current labor force worked to support the retirements of the generation before them. It wasn't just generational theft, it was generational slavery.

Current retirees were not entirely at fault for their theft. They had been forced by Big Government policies onto the plantation of entitlement programs, unable, even if willing, to go it on their own unless they were extremely wealthy. They do, however, deserve some blame for never once voting for a candidate, either in the primaries or general election, who would have saved them from pending serfdom. They had reserved their ticket on the Titanic and never once tried to change ships.

The iceberg that was going to sink entitlement programs, and with it the country, was looming menacingly in the near future. The only thing that would have stopped the coming apocalypse was a refusal to raise the debt ceiling, which would have brought about an immediate balanced budget and an end to unstainable borrowing.

It would also have meant drastic cuts to Social Security and Medicare, something that no politician would ever be willing to do. The reality, however, is that by doing nothing, these programs were eventually eliminated on a timetable not of our own choosing. These foolish promises we made to ourselves were going to be broken—it was just a question of whether it would be in a voluntarily and managed default or an involuntary, unmanageable one brought about by economic collapse.

As the future soon revealed, the former would have been greatly preferable. If Congress would have had the courage to refuse to raise the debt ceiling, I would not be rotting in a prison cell right now but would be home with you as fall turns to winter.

I always loved autumn in Iowa—the cool, crisp mornings, the smell of burning leaves, deer and pheasant hunting, the promise of snow in the air. I confess that sometimes I fear that I may never again be able to experience nature's joys with you. What we had originally thought would be a short stint as a prisoner of war has now turned into a lifetime.

Despair constantly presses in around us and, if we are not careful, will get the better of us. It is only by prayer and camaraderie that my men and I are able to keep hope alive as despondency descends upon us. Christmas will soon be upon us, and we desperately hope it doesn't find us still imprisoned and apart from our loved ones. If a prisoner exchange does not occur soon, it is our hope to escape to spend Christmas at home.

I love you greatly, and please know that you are constantly in my thoughts and prayers.

Your affectionate grandfather,
Col. Peter Iossi

LETTER X

MY DEAREST GRANDCHILDREN,

It began with a cough. Corporal Tim Robinson, housed several cells down the hall from me, had been rather sickly since I last wrote. He was prone to coughing fits, developed both a fever and chills, was extremely fatigued, and had lost a considerable amount of weight. We alerted the guards who, rather than transferring him to the prison infirmary, forced him to join the rest of us in the exercise room for our one hour of activity a day.

The sound of his coughing was horrific, his body writhing in obvious pain. We tried to comfort him and loaned him our shirts to keep him warm, but all in vain. His condition worsened, and eventually he began spitting up blood during his forced excursions to the exercise room. It finally got him the medical attention he needed, but it was too late for the corporal. He died a few days later from tuberculosis.

We have no idea where he got it from, or yet who, if anyone, he has given it to. It can take several days or weeks (or even longer) for the disease to develop, so now it becomes a waiting game. Thankfully none of us appear to have any of the corporal's symptoms, but every sneeze, cough, sniffle, or fever is looked at warily.

We could be tested for the disease and given medication, but the guards, for reasons unbeknownst to us, have shown no interest in doing so. There is rampant speculation that the only reason they have no desire to prevent a t.b. epidemic is because the prisoner-exchange talks have broken down, though we yet have no way to confirm this.

With Thanksgiving fast approaching, it breaks my heart that I will likely be spending it in Cell No. 73 miles away from those I love most. As you eat the turkey, watch football games, and decorate for Christmas, pause to remember why we celebrate it. As the pilgrims did long ago, it is time for us as families and as a nation to thank Providence for His provisions in our lives.

True, it does seem like there may not be much to

be thankful for this year with the war and all it has cost us. But God is providing us a new nation, with a new birth of freedom and the promise of peace in the years to come. And we have each other, without which we would be adrift on the sea of life. There will always be evil and sorrow in life, but it can either defeat us or it can strengthen our faith for the future.

Shortly after Obama's reelection, around Thanksgiving of 2012, a number of people from a multitude of states signed secession petitions filed with the White House. Signing such petitions were a risky proposition, as names were remembered and arrests were made in the years to come.

Even if successful, however, the effort would have been for naught in 2012. For even if the federal government had allowed states to peacefully secede, it is dubious that the people in the seceding states would have turned away from the socialist policies of the past century. In their greed, they would have continued to live off of other people's money, eventually running up a debt that would rival that of the country they were withdrawing from.

The seceding states would have been more conservative, certainly, but they were also still addicted to Big Government. In the end, gradually at first and then with rapid acceleration, they would have become the Leviathan they thought they were fleeing. As the future revealed, it is sometimes only by hitting bottom that people stop pretending and begin to see their true predicament. It doesn't have to be this way, but it too often is.

Still, a delayed Leviathan may have been better than the one we found ourselves in during Obama's second term. Like the Chicago politician he is, Obama used his second term to exact revenge on his political opponents. He put many a Republican-owned company out of business by refusing them loans, permits, licensing, and government contracts.

His bureaucracy developed a sadistic pleasure in finding and prosecuting companies and individuals for even the slightest infractions of obscure regulations passed by federal agencies, rather than Congress. Your great-uncle Jacob Iossi was fined several million dollars after a federal SWAT team raided his guitar business for allegedly violating India law in importing wood from that country. Though India itself said that there was no law violation, Jacob's company was found guilty and later had to declare bankruptcy.

Jacob himself managed to avoid personal bankruptcy, only to find himself in trouble with the IRS. Of all of Obama's weapons against his opponents, this was the one he loved the most. The IRS would audit, re-audit, and re-audit again until they found something to prosecute an outspoken critic of the Obama Administration for. Jacob settled with the IRS out-of-court for an undisclosed sum of money, but many others were not so fortunate and found themselves accused of trumped up tax evasion charges.

Many of these unfortunate souls pled guilty to lessor charges rather than risk a trial and conviction of more serious charges with lengthy prison sentences. It was an unfair fight from the beginning — individuals with limited means against a massive bureaucracy of unlimited resources, time, agents, and lawyers threatening sentences that were, in effect, life sentences if found guilty. The risk was too great, prompting many to cut their loses and plead to far more lenient sentences.

Unfortunately, because many were millionaires with names people didn't recognize, few cared about what was happening. Congress did try to exercise some oversight of the sprawling, unelected bureaucracy, but it soon became clear that such oversight was in name only. The White House ignored or stonewalled congressional subpoenas, often hiding under claims of executive privilege.

Even if wrongdoing was found, it was impossible to find a majority in a divided Congress to censure the officials involved, much less write new legislation to prevent it from happening in the future. Even if it controlled both chambers of Congress, the minority party was never able to overcome the threat of presidential veto. And, of course, the Department of Justice rarely prosecuted federal officials for the abuse and corruption of their positions.

The Obama bureaucracy issued more new regulations during his two terms in office then the previous 43 presidents did combined. To save money, the government merely posted them online rather than print the endless volumes. The government was required to calculate the costs of these regulations on the economy, but the Obama Administration eventually stopped doing so because the price tag was too shocking.

Congress increasingly found its lawmaking authority slowly ceded to the president, who would issue a law, call it a regulation, and selectively enforce it. And because it lacked a veto-proof majority in both chambers to overturn the regulation with an actual law, Congress could do nothing but whine and complain. The imperial presidency that would wreck havoc on the country in years to come had finally shown its ugly head.

If a politician tells you he cares, tell him to quit and join the Salvation Army or the Red Cross. The universal law of government is that it cannot care except by using someone else's money. And their caring always causes disproportionally unforeseen and adverse reactions that will require yet further regulations to "correct." It is a cycle that never ends and is excruciatingly difficult for a society to extradite itself from.

Unfortunately, President Obama was proud that his healthcare law was called ObamaCare because, he fondly boasted, he really did care about people. In retrospect, those same voters now likely wish he hadn't cared so much. In Obama's second term, medical costs soared, doctors became scarce, and going to the Department of Motor Vehicles was a more pleasurable experience than a routine doctor visit.

Under ObamaCare, thousands of companies across the United States found it cheaper to reduce substantial portions of their work force to part-time hours. Millions of workers suddenly found themselves only working 20-30 hours a week and without health insurance, nor with any money to pay for it. ObamaCare provided them with subsidies (i.e., other people's money) to buy insurance, but fewer and fewer doctors were willing to take patients with a government-approved health insurance plan.

The dilemma faced by these workers and the soaring costs of subsidies prompted Congress once again to enact health care "reform." But rather than recognize the failure of government compassion, Congress moved one step closer to full government-run healthcare. While Medicare remained available for seniors, Medicaid was expanded for everyone else who didn't have employer-provided health insurance. Additionally, doctors who took patients with private insurance also had to take those with either Medicaid or Medicare.

This legislation, passed in Obama's last year in office, was hardly a solution. The federal government continued to "reform" the system every other year or so, but the only change we saw was for the worse. Of course, we were assured that this was never the government's fault, but entirely that of the "greedy private sector that preys on the weak and helpless." The private sector was demonized, made into the ogre of childhood nightmares.

Obama was never much of a fan of the private sector, which suffered under his administration, especially with millions of new part-time workers caused by ObamaCare. When the government sector becomes big enough to be labeled its own "sector," it never bodes well for that other sector called the economy. It used to be said that when Detroit sneezed, the economy caught a cold. In the mixed economy of the 21st century, however, if Washington sneezed, the economy would develop pneumonia.

In an economy with consistently high unemployment and large numbers of part–time workers, people soon discovered that their college degrees weren't worth the paper they were printed on, much less the tens of thousands of dollars they spent for them. Millions of unemployed or underemployed recent college graduates were unable to repay their student loans, resulting in widespread defaults across the country. Naturally, the federal government stepped in and bailed them out...with $1 trillion of new debt.

Though not without problems of her own, China had become the world's largest economy by the end of Obama's second term. Hong Kong and London surpassed New York as the financial centers of the world, with an increasing number of Fortune 500 companies relocating oversees in order to avoid the increasing taxes and regulations imposed on American businesses. Absent the luxury of being able to relocate, many small businesses had no choice but to close under the crushing weight of Big Government.

The stagnant economy was, of course, blamed on the evil, dysfunctional free market that needed yet more government intervention to police it and make it grow. Despite several more stimulus packages and endless rounds of printing money by the Federal Reserve, nothing went up except the national debt. Medicare and Social Security—along with stimuluses, the student loan bailout, the failed ObamaCare, and the newly expanded Medicaid program—pushed the national debt to $25 trillion by the end of Obama's second term.

More ominously, interest on the debt (the amount we had to pay each year or default on our loans) doubled to $500 billion a year. Given that federal revenues went entirely to the black hole of entitlement spending, we had to borrow yet more money just to pay our debt interest. We tried to increase the interest rates we were paying on our treasury bonds to lure skittish lenders, but this only increased the amount of money we had to borrow.

When a minority of both Republicans and Democrats threatened to block yet another raise in the debt ceiling, President Obama used it as a pretext to act on his own. Arguing that he had the constitutional authority to see that the country's bills were paid, Obama suspended the debt ceiling indefinitely and ordered his Treasury secretary to continue issuing bonds to pay the bills when they came due. Congress, as usual, whined but did nothing else, and the president's illegal actions were later ratified by an Obama-packed Supreme Court.

Along with more debt came, predictably, more taxes. By the end of Obama's second term, Republicans had agreed to raise taxes rates by ten percent on those making over $250,000 a year. Some resisted, but most feared being portrayed as pawns of the rich in the midst of a presidential election year. Though popular with the voters, the increased taxes only paid for eighteen hours of federal government spending.

Along with more debt and more taxes came, just as predictably, little to no spending cuts. President Obama considered entitlements sacred promises to ourselves that he wouldn't touch, even for generations that were still years from receiving them. Similarly, spending on stimulus packages, education, infrastructure, etc. were treated as sacrosanct "investments in the future." The only thing he would, and did, cut was the military, with the 2016 budget reducing the growth in defense spending by half in ten years. As it would turn out, the defense department would be overjoyed if that was all that was cut.

Early in Obama's second term, my team and I were in Iraq tracking shipments of weapons of mass destruction from the collapsing regime of Syrian President Assad to Iran. We were near Baghdad one night when we learned that the US embassy was being attacked by a heavily armed mob. We asked permission to go to the aid of our staff there, but were informed that the president had given orders for all assets in the region to stand down.

We refused. By morning we had moved the embassy personnel to a secure location, though we lost one civilian and two of my men in the process. Inexplicably, the White House never sought to have their bodies returned to U.S. soil. We were applauded as unnamed heros, with the president naturally taking credit for our actions.

Though we had disobeyed a direct order, the president couldn't discipline us for fear that the world would learn of his cowardice. So he transferred us from special forces back to the 1st Division where we would be unable to embarrass him again. It was just as well, as I was happy to be home more and have some normalcy in my life. It was also during this time that I managed to finish law school at night in between your father's basketball games and violin lessons. I wasn't sure if I would ever actually practice law, but I never like to leave a job unfinished.

I must close for now. As always, please know that I miss you terribly and long to see you soon. I am eternally thankful for you and pray for you constantly.

Your affectionate grandfather,
Col. Peter Iossi

LETTER XI

MY DEAREST GRANDCHILDREN,

I hope you had a wonderful Thanksgiving back home in Iowa. Much to our unhappy surprise, our guards were feeling particularly festive and provided each floor with a turkey to celebrate the holiday. A single bird was insufficient to feed an entire floor, but we were hardly in a position to turn down such a gift.

As always, however, the generosity of our captors was for their amusement at our expense. Floor by floor we were escorted to the prison yard where we found a live turkey running in wild fright in the cold, snow covered yard. We were told to catch our meal ourselves and that, if unsuccessful, we would be given a diet of live rats once again.

So despite the freezing temperatures and the unplowed five inches of freshly fallen snow on the ground, we took off after the fowl creature. It wasn't easy, but after nearly an hour of futile scrambling we finally caught our Thanksgiving dinner. Then the real cruelty began as the guards lit a bonfire with which to cook the turkey. Shivering in only our prison uniforms and bare feet, we were eagerly looking forward to warming ourselves by the fire. But the guards, while toasting themselves by the blaze, kept us from approaching closer than fifty yards.

Finally, after intentionally overcooking the turkey to the point that it was dry and tasteless, we were told to get in a circle around the bird and, on the count of "tres," outrace our fellow soldiers for a slice of turkey dinner. Though we jogged towards the turkey, we maintained discipline and ordered ourselves in a single-file line of ascending rank, with each solider taking a portion. Despite barely weighing twelve pounds dripping wet, we were frugal enough with the turkey to ensure that everyone had a few morsels to eat.

Much to the guards' annoyance, each floor similarly performed selflessly and orderly when commanded by the guards to fight each other for their turkey. Robbed of the sight of seeing us brawling, the enraged guards placed us on a diet of live rats for a week. Adding to their cruelty, they gave us the rats all at once, flooding Cell No. 73 with 168 of the vile rodents.

We were finally able to capture and kill them all, but not until after a lengthy and ugly battle. As before, we didn't eat them but flushed them one by one down the toilet until it became backed up from every other cell doing the same thing. Having no other option, we tossed the remaining dead rats back through the cell door, where presumably they were collected and made into next week's "Tex-Mex." At least this way, however, they would be cooked.

Two of my three cellmates have developed tuberculosis, as has roughly half of the prison population. Given the lack of space in the prison hospital to treat them all, only those on their death beds are housed there. The rest are given antibiotics, but otherwise left unattended to in their cells. The sound of a cough, sneeze, or blowing nose constantly echoes in the air, making it nearly impossible to sleep soundly.

My sick cellmates remain in our cell, shivering and huddling under their worn bedsheets stained with rat feces. My healthy cellmate and I have loaned them our sheets in an effort to stop the shivering, but nothing seems to warm them up. The guards do not force them to make the excursion to the exercise room each day, but they were required to enjoy the outside Thanksgiving festivities with the rest of us. Needless to say, the mental and physical toll they experienced that day has caused their condition to deteriorate substantially.

Please do not worry about me. I have yet to show any signs of tuberculosis, and believe that the epidemic has nearly run its course. They refuse to test the healthy ones for the disease or give us antibiotics but, since I have yet to show any symptoms, it appears that I may have a natural defense to it. But please pray for the sick here, as the medical care is atrocious and the death toll continues to mount. As of last count, twenty prisoners have died from the cursed disease.

Death tolls of a different sort were an increasingly tragic topic of conversation in the 2016 presidential election. With rapidly increasing frequency during Obama's second term, mass shootings would occur at schools, malls, restaurants, churches, and places of work. They were acts of terrorism, shed of any ideology or agenda except random and meaningless carnage.

Unlike the War on Terrorism which was fought

against identifiable Muslim terrorists, this terrorism lived among us and could only be identified by the term "evil." It was one thing to live in a country such as Israel and face constant suicide bombers and rocket attacks and know who the enemy is and that it is not you. It was quite another, however, for America to live in constant fear of terrorist attacks from a nameless evil within.

After years of a cradle-to-grave welfare state that was supposed to protect them from the hardships of life, the electorate demanded swift government action to restore their troubled Matrix. America refused to recognize that this evil was the natural byproduct of an increasingly godless society that killed its own young in the womb, nor did it understand that such evil could only be stopped by a moral course correction. It wasn't a gun problem, but a moral one—Americans, having forsaken a belief in Absolute Truth, no longer possessed the inner moral restraints to control their behavior.

Rather than face the demon within, however, the public demanded to ban the tools of evil rather than the conditions that encouraged it in the first place. But there are no steps that can be taken to disarm evil, for it will always find a way to wreck mayhem and ruin. A disarmed society only makes it easier for evil to prevail, while one armed with virtue and bullets can effectively keep it at bay.

The presidential nominee of the Democrat Party made gun control the major issue of his campaign, conveniently pushing uncomfortable issues like the budget and debt off the table. His campaign slogan was simple—"Safe homes, safe streets, safe schools." He promised peace in exchange for partial disarmament, and he won in a landslide.

Despite frantic public demand, Congress found itself deadlocked and unable to pass any gun control legislation. The president, emboldened by his resounding electoral mandate, bypassed Congress altogether and imposed gun control by executive order. His presidential fiat renewed the 1994 "assault weapons" ban and banned the sale of magazine clips that could hold more than ten bullets.

He prohibited individuals from carrying guns in public buildings, parks, schools, businesses, and churches, leaving people free to walk armed only in their homes and on the street. He also ordered the registration of all gun owners and gun/hunting groups, and made it possible for gun manufacturers to be exposed to civil liability for the deaths and injurers caused by their weapons.

Additionally, the president created a federal buy-back program in which the government purchased guns at current market value, no questions asked. By lacking a requirement that individuals prove they owned the guns they were turning in, the program only encouraged the theft of firearms from law-abiding citizens in order to make a few bucks. These robberies, of course, were conveniently never reported in the media nor investigated by authorities.

The returned guns were then burned in public displays around the country to appease the public's pent up anger at the violence that threatened their utopia. Nearly a century before Hitler came to power, an astute German remarked that when a society burns books, they will ultimately burn people. The same, America found out too late, could be said about guns.

The president also prohibited those diagnosed with mental illnesses from owning firearms. In order to screen potential homicidal threats, the president required mental health examinations for all those graduating from kindergarten, elementary, middle, and high schools, and any post-secondary institution. He also required employers to ensure that their employees had an annual mental health exam. As the future would tragically reveal, those who defined what a mental illness was would in effect determine who could and could not exercise a full-range of constitutional rights.

Paranoid that anyone with a mental illness may be the next mass murderer, family members, neighbors, co-workers, and fellow students reported anyone with the oddest behavior or statements to the mental health authorities. Initially laws were passed that exposed individuals to civil negligence if they failed to report such an individual, but these quickly became federal requirements punishable by criminal sanctions.

In addition to the metal detectors and large security forces maintained by schools, colleges, public buildings, and many places of business, street cameras and drones became all too common. Cities and towns used to measure security by the number of police officers they had on payroll, but now they did so by the number of drones in their hanger. At first they were unarmed and merely used for surveillance, but that soon changed in the years to come.

America became one giant police state in which one could never hide from the lidless, ever vigilant eye of Big Government. But despite all these measures, no one felt safe, and, to no one's real surprise, the shootings increased rather than decreased. Only the law-abiding citizens obeyed these restrictions, while criminals disregarded them at will.

Upon my encouragement, my family members became responsible and experienced gun owners who carried handguns in public as much as they could. My father-in-law, your great-grandfather Michael, was able to stop a mass shooter in his nursing home with his 9 mm. While heralded a hero, guns were thereafter prohibited in nursing homes for visitors, workers, and residents alike.

Because of their low security presence, nursing homes became attractive targets for mass murderers who cared far more about shooting the immobile residents inside than the little "no weapons allowed" sticker on the front door. Refusing to surrender his right to self-defense to someone else, Michael kept his 9 mm and used it the following year to stop yet another mass shooting in his nursing home. He was arrested and charged with violating federal law, but thankfully a jury declined to convict a two-time hero.

The president's executive orders were praised in Congress, applauded by the public, and upheld in court against legal challenges to executive lawmaking. The president argued, and the Supreme Court agreed, that the nation's chief executive had the inherent constitutional authority to act on behalf of the general welfare in cases of national emergencies when Congress was gridlocked. The rise of the presidency as a de facto elective monarchy was nearly complete; the era of congressional lawmaking was effectively over.

Nearly two-hundred and fifty years after throwing off the British monarchy, the American people found themselves embracing a Caesar who would finally get things done in Washington. They had grown weary of constant congressional bickering that threatened fiscal cliffs, defaults, government shutdowns, and other horribles that might threaten their government benefits. They cared more for the successful administration of the welfare, nanny state than they did for constitutional niceties.

But for all his power, the new Caesar could do nothing about the economic morass the country was in. All the government programs, stimulus packages, and regulations only resulted in stagnant economic growth with unemployment levels hovering around ten percent. But rather than acknowledge that government was the problem rather than the solution, the president simply increased the government management of the private sector.

In an effort to turn a profit, businesses cut

expenses by no longer providing health insurance to any of their employees, dumping millions of Americans on to the rolls of the newly-expanded Medicaid program. A few health insurance companies made an attempt to offer plans for the wealthy, but the government quickly eliminated any form of competition. The health care industry was, for all practical purposes, nationalized. It may still have been performed by private doctors and hospitals, but it was under the command and control of the government.

By 2018, countless states, counties, and municipalities were facing bankruptcy because of their uncontrollable spending, threatening the jobs of millions of government workers and the pensions of tens of millions already retired. The federal government, naturally, stepped in to bail them out to the tune of $6 trillion. No one cared about the price tag, however, because catastrophe had been adverted.

Besides, by this point both the political class and the media had convinced the public that deficit government spending had only positive, not negative, effects on the country's economic health. It was necessary, they were told, to spur economic growth and that each dollar the government spent magically turned into two dollars in the private sector. Instead of $6 trillion of new debt, the public was convinced that $12 trillion of economic growth had been created.

Of course, all this government spending caused the national debt to rise to $32 trillion dollars. America was spending $1.5 trillion a year just to keep up with the interest on its debt, with rates at or above Greece-like levels of 13%. This higher interest rate had a trickle down effect, making it much more difficult for individuals and businesses to borrow money at rates they could afford.

Increasingly, the Federal Reserve became the only buyer to show up at our treasury auctions to buy our new bonds with newly created money. Though other countries, for the most part, declined to sell their current bonds, they refused to continue to buy new ones to finance our spendthrift ways. Inevitably, all the new money created by the Fed to "stimulate" the economy was exceeding demand, causing inflation to rise near ten percent.

In an effort to reduce the country's annual $2 trillion budget deficits, Congress raised taxes on household making over $50,000 a year by five percent. Surprisingly few people objected, largely because most were no longer working or were making too little to be effected. Those in households making between $50,000 and $70,000 a year, however, were shocked to learn that they were no longer considered middle class but classified with the wealthy.

They suddenly found themselves on the wrong side of the slippery slope of progressive taxation, but nobody cared. It reminded me of a famous quote by Martin Niemöller, an anti-Nazi German pastor imprisoned under Hitler. Paraphrasing for context, he wrote:

> First they came for the wealthiest one-percent, and I didn't speak out because I wasn't a one-percenter.
>
> Then they came for the top two-percent, and I didn't speak out because I wasn't a two-percenter.
>
> Then they came for the top ten percent, and I didn't speak out because I wasn't a ten-percenter.
>
> Then they came for me, and nobody cared nor could offer a defense.

The year 2020 was an election year and, despite the sweeping new regulations, they had no affect in curtailing the incidents of mass shootings. Seeking reelection, the president feared the public would blame him for the mounting death toll from the uncontrollable violence, resulting in 220 mass shooting deaths in 2020 alone. So, as all politicians are wont to do, he blamed it on something else—hate speech.

Claiming that the violence was due to the poisonous atmosphere created by offensive language, he issued an executive order prohibiting any speech that incited discrimination, hostility, or violence. The ban, upheld by the courts, became criminally enforced political correctness that the Left used to effectively silence its opponents. Any speaker critical of groups or policies favored by liberals was immediately investigated by the Department of Justice.

Churches, in particular, found themselves gagged by this executive order, hesitant in calling many behaviors sin for fear of offending sinners who would in turn report them to the authorities. Adultery, fornication, pornography, homosexuality, alcoholism, and gambling were among the many topics churches were told not to discuss. It was still permissible, for the time being, to believe in God, absolute Truth, natural rights, objective right and wrong, and repentance and judgment, but it was becoming increasingly difficult to express those convictions publicly. The notion of sinners in the hands of an angry God made too many sinners a tad too uncomfortable.

Secession, naturally, also became a forbidden topic. Anyone who publicly advocated secession as a viable alternative faced potential prosecution for treason. Secession may have occurred without bloodshed in 2012 if a group of states actually had the fortitude to go through with it, for it was unlikely that war-hating, gun-hating liberals would have marched to war to prevent it, nor would they have had much popular support.

By 2020, however, liberals and their entitlement-dependent constituencies understood that if secession were successful, it would see the diminishment of their tax base. They also feared that anyone with any money and common sense within their borders would be tempted to join the greener pastures of the seceding states, forcing them to build their own version of the Berlin Wall. For the love of other people's money, therefore, they would gladly have resorted to military force to keep it from walking away.

Bored with being part of an army that never fought because the nation couldn't afford it, I retired from the service with the rank of lieutenant colonel shortly before the presidential election. To provide excuses for reducing the nation's military power in order to pay for the ever increasing entitlement spending, the president had, in part, blamed the country's "martial spirit" and "warmongering" for creating the culture that led to the mass shootings. Seeing its budget shrivel to levels below that of China and Russia, the military was largely reduced to humanitarian missions; a Red Cross with guns.

Upon "retirement," I returned to Iowa to open my own law practice, deciding that criminal defense was where the trench warfare over the Constitution was taking place. In the face of the tyranny and oppression I saw around me, I wanted to stand between the state and its prey and say, "This far and no further unless and until you can prove your case beyond a reasonable doubt without violating my client's constitutional rights."

Often the state could easily prove that the law was violated, but I built up a practice defending those accused of hate speech by asking juries to nullify the law. Jury nullification is the ancient tradition that the jury, as representatives of the sovereign people, could refuse to enforce a law they considered unjust. Courts, however, often sanctioned me for urging it, declaring that they were the sole judges of a law's constitutionality. But I never had a jury, after learning that they could nullify the 2020 hate speech edict, refuse to do so.

I must close for now. There are no signs of any pending prisoner exchange, and we are growing restless with despair. If nothing happens soon, we hope to make a prison break before Christmas. Just the thought of being home with you in time for Christmas makes my eyes water and my heart ache with longing. But we must be prudent and patient, keeping our emotions in check to avoid doing something fatally careless.

So I must close with much long-suffering hope, love, and prayers until I can write (or see you) again.

Your affectionate grandfather,
Col. Peter Iossi

LETTER XII

MY DEAREST GRANDCHILDREN,

Today is Christmas, and I am still here in Cell No. 73. It turns out that I do not have any natural defenses to tuberculosis after all, which ironically saved my life. Because of my illness, I was unable to join the few healthy among us in a prison escape that tragically ended up costing them their lives.

Only seven men were healthy enough to make the attempt, and all but one were captured and executed. They had made it several miles beyond the prison walls, but months of malnourishment and little exercise left them unable to outrun the pursuit. They were brought back and, while the rest of us were forced to watch, hung on the unused gallows from September, their bodies left hanging to rot in the prison yard.

The one who managed to get away was my healthy cellmate, Captain William Manning. He was always a natural athlete and a gifted runner, winning gold in the marathon several years ago at the 2028 summer olympics in Moscow. Surviving in the wild in the winter, however, requires an entirely different set of skills, but I pray that he makes it to your place before this letter does.

Unlike Thanksgiving, our guards appear more interested in getting drunk then by celebrating the holiday with any cruel festivities. They won't get any complaints from my men, most of whom are too sick to have played their games even if they wanted to. My condition is holding steady at tolerable, though at times my coughing becomes uncontrollable. Despite the medication we receive, far too many are in far worse shape than I am, and the death toll now approaches forty.

In addition to saving my life, the disease has given me the most vivid dreams of Christmases past as I restlessly sleep the time and misery away. Did I ever tell you about the birth of your father Jonathan? We were spending Christmas with my in-laws, the aforementioned two-time mass shooting hero Michael and his wife Rebecca, near their rural home in western Michigan.

Fueled by the lake effect as it sped towards us across Lake Michigan, a blizzard threatened to make it a very white and very snowbound Christmas holed up with Michael and Rebecca for several days. Though your grandmother Sarah was quite pregnant at the time, we weren't too concerned because Jonathan wasn't due for another ten days.

As was his wont, however, he preferred to get a jump start on life rather than idle time away. We tried to make it to the nearest hospital thirty minutes away, but not even Michael's 4-by-4 diesel pickup truck with chains on its tires could navigate a path through the blizzard. Fortunately, an obstetrician lived a few hundred yards away from my in-laws and, after a few adventures of his own, made it in time to help deliver Jonathan at 4:22 that Christmas afternoon in 2000.

Today would've marked his 34th birthday and, while I miss him terribly, I know that he and your grandmother are in a far better place. They wouldn't trade their new home for this one even if given the chance, and neither will I once my feet reach that far heavenly shore. Understanding that this world is but a fleeting whisper, but that eternity lasts forever, puts this life with all its cares and priorities in perspective.

In 2000, however, the cares of this world didn't appear all that troublesome when the national debt was only a few trillion dollars and our present troubles barely appeared as a black cloud in the distant and completely avoidable future. By 2022, however, that black cloud became the present as American insolvency became its harsh new reality.

The national debt had, by the first of that year, reached an unfathomable $40 trillion. With rates at 25%, the interest payments America had to make on its debt each year totaled $2.5 trillion, roughly 60% of all tax revenue. Together, interest payments and entitlement spending alone amounted to $7.5 trillion a year, with other government spending on such things as infrastructure, education, and the military totaled another $2 trillion annually.

Finally, our lenders had had enough. For the past decade, the Federal Reserve had been one of the few foolish buyers of new U.S. bonds, financing three-quarters of the $24 trillion of debt America had racked up since 2012. As fewer and fewer countries used the dollar to trade in, however, all this newly printed money vastly exceeded demand, causing inflation to reach 20% with no signs of slowing down.

A number of countries and institutions who had

bought our treasury bonds before 2012 were growing frustrated at being paid with increasingly worthless US dollars. The return on investment wasn't worth the risk they ran that America would soon default, leaving them with neither interest nor principle.

So on Super Bowl Sunday they informed the chairman of the Federal Reserve that they would sell off their bonds the following morning...unless the parties could come to an understanding. Such a selloff would lead to a run on treasury bonds and, simultaneously, a run on the dollar, leading to an immediate and crushing economic collapse.

The chairman had no choice but to acquiesce to their demands. Unlike Greece in 2012, there was no one big enough to bail us out of our $40 trillion debt crises. Neither could we refinance our $40 trillion mortgage, especially with worthless money. Nor could we continue to print more money to buy new bonds or pay off old ones without causing Zimbabwe-like hyperinflation.

Neither could we simply repudiate our debt and start over with a balanced budget, for we were long past the era in which we could live within our means. By 2022, every American was dependent on the federal government for health insurance, and roughly half the population was dependent for their basic necessities on programs such as Social Security, disability insurance, unemployment benefits, food stamps, etc.

All this entitlement spending totaled $5 trillion a year which, even in a good tax year, exceeded all federal revenue. More debt, therefore, was necessary to continue to finance our welfare nation. Borrowing more money at affordable rates, however, would be next to impossible if we repudiated our existing debt and left current lenders with trillions of dollars in loses. It would be years before our credit rating would ever recover from such a self-inflicted blow, which would be far too late to prevent total societal collapse brought on by a sudden and abrupt end to the nation's entitlement programs.

So the Fed chairman arranged a managed default on our debt that allowed us to maintain, for the time being, some degree of credit worthiness and thereby continue the necessary deficit spending to finance the entitlement state. The nations who had loaned us money would not budge—refusing to agree to a buyout, refinance, or repayment in either inflated dollars or a new US currency.

Instead, they would only consider our debt satisfactorily repaid if we did so with something far more tangible than fiat money; an in-kind exchange of goods for solvency. China, for instance, was given our public utilities and energy infrastructure on a silver platter. Japan was given title (and hence all royalty rights) to 70% of all interior federal lands.

Taiwan was given all rights and royalties to oil drilling along our coasts, and Brazil received Puerto Rico and the Virgin Islands. Russia, who had strategically enhanced its holdings of US debt for this very reason, was given all federal lands and royalty rights in Alaska, which amounted to 65% of the state. Naturally, Americans had to pay these royalties and fees in the currencies of the respective countries rather than dollars.

Despite this national emasculation and shame, our national debt still wasn't entirely paid off because of the trillions of dollars we owed to private investors, banks, public institutions, pension funds, and mutual funds. To prevent these investors from starting a run on treasury bonds, the Federal Reserve agreed to purchase their shares at face value. The Fed than agreed to refinance all the bonds it held, rolling them over into staggered 50-year notes at 0% interest.

We also continued to owe trillions of dollars to ourselves in the form of IOUs to "intergovernmental trust funds" (i.e., government pensions, Social

Security, Medicare, etc.). The problem, however, is that for years these trust funds had told the American people that the money was there and that the funds were solvent.

The honest thing would have been to cancel the debt to the trust funds and eliminate them altogether and to continue to pay for entitlement spending directly out of the treasury without the charade. But this would have entailed too much truth for the American people, who would suddenly see that their retirements were not being paid for out of their "lock box" stored in a government vault in West Virginia but from their children's tax dollars. Such naked generational theft would not have sat well with the public, so nothing at all was done with this intergovernmental debt.

In order to keep inflation from becoming rampant, the Fed chair needed to find a way to keep demand for the dollar high by encouraging countries to continue to use it in trading with each other. The OPEC nations agreed to continue to use the dollar when trading oil, but only after we agreed to recognize Palestinian statehood and no longer interfere in the domestic affairs of the Islamic world. Great Britain, Germany, and Japan also agreed to continue to use the dollar in international trade, but only after we removed all duties on the goods we imported from them.

By the time the dust cleared late that Super Bowl Sunday 2022, the rise of inflation had been halted and the only debt we owed was to the trust funds and the zero interest bonds held by the Federal Reserve. When the agreement was announced the following morning, the Fed chairman was heralded a genius, praised as the savior of his country, and named Man of the Year. Congress even declared a national holiday after him.

However, because we needed to start issuing new treasury bonds to finance our welfare state, we had to persuade investors that we were serious about reducing deficit spending. There were two ways to do this—cutting entitlement spending or raising taxes. We attempted both.

We made cosmetic changes to entitlement spending, but not enough to control costs. The retirement age was gradually raised to 70 for those 54 and younger, and Social Security and Medicare were means-tested so that the rich received less benefits. But medical costs continued to soar, which, naturally, meant the deficit did too.

While the cuts in spending were largely superficial, the taxes were real. In the name of making the "rich" pay their "fair share," income above $50,000 was taxed at 55% and income above $200,000 was taxed at 75%. After all, the nation was told, if the poor had to sacrifice a few extra years of labor before they could retire, the "rich" should have to sacrifice a few extra percentage points of income. Never mind that these "rich" also had to sacrifice the equal number of years of extra labor before they could participate in the same retirement programs, albeit with considerably fewer benefits so that the poor could have more.

A "modest" national sales tax of 3% was introduced, but there were so many items excluded that those making under $50,000 were hardly effected. In an effort to find new revenue streams, Congress legalized prostitution, gambling, obscene pornography, and most narcotics for the sole purpose of being able to tax them. In an effort to import legal, taxable employees, Congress granted blanket amnesty to illegal immigrants already in the country and offered tax incentives to encourage highly educated immigrants to relocate here.

Finally, the president sought to find more revenue by sending his Department of Justice after big businesses and their owners for even the slightest infraction of the most inconsequential regulation in

117

order to levy huge fines on them.   This used to be done as a form of political payback, but now was done as a routine means of raising money. The IRS also began auditing every third household who made more than $50,000 in a naked shakedown to wring more money out of them.

Of course, all this new revenue did little to stop the deficit spending, but that was for the president's successor to deal with. The current president, who had been reelected in 2020, was too occupied with his self-appointed but largely unfulfilled legacy as the man who ended gun violence in America. Despite the gun regulations and his 2020 hate speech edict, mass shootings continued unabated, averaging at least one a month. Nearly a thousand people had died from mass shootings under his presidency, a substantial number of them children.

In further attempts to stop the carnage, the president exposed any speaker who offended someone to civil liability for the negligent infliction of emotional distress. With precious few exceptions, opinion media, whether on television, radio, or the internet, went silent overnight. Only "news accounts" were exempted under the law and, of course, it was the president and his Department of Justice who determined what the news was and how it could be reported.

Churches were not exempted from this new edict under the theory that a person's religious rights do not give them a license to offensive hate speech. Religion, the courts held, must yield to the right of others not to be offended. In order to avoid bankruptcy, therefore, pastors began to require visitors to sign waivers releasing them from civil liability and, when the courts found these to be invalid, limited their services to church members only.

A number of churches, however, refused to be silenced, believing that God had commanded them to boldly preach the Gospel "into all the world." A remarkable thing happened among these churches, for when the pastor could no longer avoid bankruptcy due to the mounting monetary damages, a lay person took to the pulpit. And when he in turn had to finally declare bankruptcy, yet another lay person took over. While penniless, these churches were joyful and actually continued to grow, while the churches who rejected the Great Commission found themselves shrinking and ineffective, amounting to little more than social clubs of hypocritical piety.

The president also enacted an edict that declared jury nullification illegal, making both those who advocated it and the juries who committed it guilty of a felony punishable by five years in prison. Undeterred in the face of tyranny, I immediately urged my next jury to nullify the 2020 hate speech law.

The case was immediately declared a mistrial (my client was later found guilty at his retrial) and I was given thirty days for contempt of court. I could have been prosecuted under the new edict, but the government didn't want to make more of a martyr out of me than necessary, especially as I was running for Congress at the time.

Knowing that I could no longer be effective as a defense attorney if I was either muzzled or in prison, I decided that the best way I could serve my country was in the political arena. Because speech by political candidates was exempted from the speech laws, I could say what I wanted without fear of bankruptcy or jail.

So in 2024 I ran on the ticket of the emerging Liberty Party, whose political slogan was borrowed from Nancy Reagan's anti-smoking campaign—"Just Say No." We didn't promise anything from the government except to protect man's natural, unalienable rights to life, liberty, and property. We didn't offer government solutions, we offered freedom from government. We didn't run on making the government run more efficient, but on letting the private sector run free and efficiently.

And while our message was overwhelmingly rejected by most Americans, there were still a few pockets where it was warmly received. Though we failed to win any statewide seats, we managed to pick up a few congressional seats in the Midwest, South, and Mountain West, including my own. A total of fourteen congressional districts across the country denounced the use of government coercion for selfish means. It was barely a start, but at least it was a start.

Nearly a decade ago now in January of 2025 I found myself being sworn in as the newest member of Iowa's congressional delegation, just in time for the long-delayed entitlement crises to erupt. But that tale must wait as I am late to attend our Christmas Day service during our daily excursion to the exercise room. I haven't felt well enough to make the trip for several weeks now, but I want to make the effort on this blessed day.

With much love and prayers until I can write (or see you) again.

> Your affectionate grandfather,
> Col. Peter Iossi

LETTER XIII

MY DEAREST GRANDCHILDREN,

Thank you for your prayers for my men and I as we continue to suffer from the vestiges of tuberculosis. The epidemic appears over and most of us, including myself, are nearly back to normal. Unfortunately, the number of men claimed by the disease now stands at fifty, most of them with young families waiting for them back home. Death in combat is one thing, but death that could have been easily prevented by proper diet and medical care is senseless cruelty.

And to compound the sorrow produced by this Second Mexican–American War, we have learned that it has suddenly turned nuclear. The Mexicans had advanced to the outskirts of Los Angeles, threatening the largest city of the newly formed Pacific States of

America (PSA). In desperation, the PSA leveled Mexico City with a half-dozen nuclear warheads, bringing an ominous stalemate across the entire front with Mexico.

No one, even the Mexicans themselves, are certain of who among their civilian and military leadership have survived. Mexico never had a real need for nuclear bunkers, even during the Cold War, and whatever bunkers existed have likely fallen into disuse and disrepair. It is doubtful that anyone among the Mexican high command made it to a bunker that could withstand such a nuclear blast.

So now we wait to see what their next move might be, and the waiting can be more unbearable than action. We are hopeful that the Mexican government will sue for peace, at least along the current battle lines or perhaps even giving us back some of the land they already conquered. Such wishful thinking, however, may well prove just that—wishful.

The Mexican army has already captured numerous nuclear weapons in its march across the south-west, and it will likely find many willing sellers on the world market as they seek to acquire more. Would they be willing to blow up a few of our cities simply to have a better seat at the bargaining table, or would they seek to exact a more punitive revenge?

And while we wait for an indication of what they might do, we curse the day the president eliminated all funding for a missile defense shield because it was too expensive. Now our cities lay naked and exposed to a ruthless neighbor seeking revenge, and the only thing we can do is deter them by the threat of mutually assured destruction.

That threat once had weight in the 20th century, but much less so now that, due to budget restraints, we decommissioned a large number of our warheads. Of those that are left, no one is sure how many will work after years of neglect and decay. It is an unfortunate reality that it is just as likely that they will blowup in their silos as it is they will hit their targets.

How did the world's sole military superpower fall so far so fast? It had survived the budget cuts under Obama and his successor, and still has an adequate budget even after the fiscal crises of 2022. But it would not survive the entitlement crises that began in ernest in 2025, when the country was forced to decide between funding its entitlement programs or its national defense. As did the socialist democracies of Western Europe before it, it did not hesitate in choosing the former.

By 2025, the United States had run out of

money...again. In the three short years since our debt problem was "solved," we had racked up $15 trillion in new debt to finance our bloated entitlement spending. Foreign and domestic lenders, having seen this drama once before, refused to continue to buy new debt. In years past the Federal Reserve would have stepped in and bought the new treasury bonds, but now it could no longer artificially increase the money supply without causing hyperinflation.

So for the first time in its history, the United States found itself unable to borrow money, forced instead to live within its means. In order to accomplish this feat that had eluded Washington for decades, the newly-elected president was forced to cut spending and raise taxes in earnest. To the surprise of no one, this lead to violent insurrection in the streets as America's day of reckoning had finally arrived.

The defense budget was the first to go, stripped to a tenth of what it was in 2012. Other departments were not spared the fiscal axe, finding their budgets cut in half with promises of more cuts to come. Only the Department of Justice, Internal Revenue Service, and the Environmental Protection Agency were spared, forced to cut only ten percent of their budgets. The administration, after all, couldn't see all of its power eaten away by budget cuts. Still, nearly half of all federal employees lost their jobs, along with millions of others in the private sector who had contracts with the government.

But for the first time in history, real cuts were made to entitlement spending. Social Security payments were cut by 40%, health care was rationed, and disability insurance, unemployment compensation, food stamps, and all other welfare programs were cut in half. The federal government no longer financed student loans, forcing instead private banks to do so with their own money. Most banks, who were frugal in loaning to Fortune 500 companies, refused to chance it with 18-year-olds and subsequently closed their doors.

On top of this, everyone saw their taxes rise considerably. The national sales tax, stripped of all exemptions, was increased to 10%, income taxes on everyone was increased 15%, and payroll taxes for such things as Social Security and Medicare were increased by 20%. Unsurprisingly, the economy not only stopped growing, but was drastically shrinking. Unemployment rose to 40% by the end of the president's first, and only, term, with inflation hovering around 30%. Trailer villages and shanty towns became the norm as the housing market failed.

Total societal collapse was upon us as the Great Depression of the 1930s began to look more and more like a minor economic hiccup. The unemployed assaulted businessmen and burned their companies to the ground in retaliation for their "greedy capitalism." The wealthy, even Hollywood celebrates and famous athletes, found their homes regularly robbed.

The young, blaming the old for fleecing their future to pay for their retirements, habitually attacked senior citizens on the street or even in retirement homes. They took particular pleasure in hunting down retired senators and congressman lying in their nursing homes, singling them out for execution for getting the country into this mess in the first place.

And everyone—young or old, working or dependents—blamed the bankers, particularly the Federal Reserve, for their misery. Its chairman, the former Man of the Year, and two of its governors were killed by a mob that stormed a meeting of the Fed. Numerous other bankers were literally tarred and feathered by angry mobs, while none escaped having their image burned in effigy by rioters.

Anti-semitism became prevalent as Jewish bankers were blamed for the economic meltdown.

Synagogues were often burned, and their rabbis arrested for inciting the violence. Entire Jewish neighborhoods in some cities were plundered by rioters. Partly out of prejudice and partly out of a desire to maintain the peace in their establishments, fewer and fewer businesses hired or served Jews. These crimes, of course, were never prosecuted.

Everyone protested everywhere—city hall, commercial districts, gas stations, grocery stores, even the farmers' market. But their favorite target were politicians, especially congressman. Often these protests would turn violent, forcing my colleagues and myself to remain on Capitol Hill behind fortified barricades. Even the president, who retreated to the relative calm of Camp David for the remainder of his term, could not escape the protestors who gathered in the hills around the compound.

He openly longed for retirement and, far from engaging in any reelection effort, actually placed a countdown calendar in the press briefing room showing the number of days until he was no longer president. He fiddled while America burned, making no effort to restore the nation's moral or economic health. By the time he left office, America was defaulting on her debt on average once every two months—choosing to pay what entitlements were left rather than the interest on its treasury bonds.

Into this void stepped the dictator, who was overwhelmingly elected president in 2028 on his pledge to restore both entitlement spending and law and order. He harnessed public anger at the rich, promising that their wealth, "accumulated at the expense of the poor," will be used to finance our continued spending.

Profits, he told the American people, were just another form of theft; the rich got rich only by making the poor poorer. But not only is wealth ill-gotten gain, he declared, it is immoral for the rich to keep it so long as there are those that go without. He argued that it was unconscionable for some to have financial security while others are in desperate need. Fairness, he told his adoring crowds, mandated not just equality of opportunity but the equality of outcomes.

His campaign slogan was "freedom from fear, freedom from want, freedom from greedy capitalists." As promised, on the very day he was inaugurated, the dictator enacted by executive order the Fair Deal, guaranteeing everyone food, health care, a job, housing, a college education, and a secure retirement, all at the public expense.

The dictator completely nationalized the health care industry in order to keep them from making profits off of other people's illnesses. While the industry had been under the command and control of the central government for decades, it had remained in private hands, if in name only. Now, however, the government owned the hospitals and clinics and their employees became federal workers. The real reason for this, of course, was to limit medical costs and ration care, but the dictator didn't tell the public that.

Similarly, the dictator nationalized all insurance industries (car, housing, flood, etc.) under the rubric that it was immoral for them to make profits off of other people's misery. What the dictator didn't tell the public, however, was that he didn't consider it immoral for the government to make profits off of such misery. Like Social Security and Medicare before it, the monthly premium payments were supposed to be deposited in a trust fund, but the dictator found it too tempting to dip into this trust fund for both public and private uses.

The Fair Deal edict created a Department of Fairness to oversee the housing czar, the jobs czar, the shared sacrifice czar (the new head of the IRS), the food czar, the Social Security Administration, and the higher education czar. While the student loan industry was once again nationalized, the Department preferred, for the time being, to keep the remaining industries in private ownership but under the command and control of the central government.

Of course, all this had to be paid for by somebody. When you can no longer either borrow money or print money, the only option left is to confiscate it. Those making under $50,000, of course, were spared the lash. The exemptions were restored to the national sales tax, and their income and payroll taxes were eliminated altogether.

But the "rich" were not so fortunate. Business profits and individual incomes over $50,000 were taxed at a rate of 90% and all their tax deductions were eliminated. After all, the dictator argued, why should they get a deduction for their mortgage when so many were homeless? And why should they get a deduction for supporting charities when the government is delivering Americans from fear or want under the Fair Deal?

The "rich" also saw their payroll taxes increase yet another 20%, while the national sales tax, which only affected them, was raised to 20%. All private retirement accounts were forcibly "rolled over" into the Social Security trust fund because, once again, it was deemed immoral for some to afford retirement while others could not.

All gold, silver, and precious jewels were confiscated by the federal government, save for wedding bands, engagement rings, and watches valued under $3,000. Sales taxes on luxury items such as high-end cars, mansions, and private planes were raised to 90%. While the sales tax on cigarettes was also raised to 90%, taxes on other vices such as prostitution and drugs were left unchanged under the theory that the poor needed their simple pleasures from the miseries of this world.

To restore law and order, the dictator declared martial law in over 70% of the country—imposing curfews and random checkpoints, declaring large areas "gun free," banning the possession of firearms outside of one's home, policing the streets with the army, and suspending the writ of habeas corpus (judicial review of arrests). Armed drones constantly patrolled the skies at all hours of the day and night. Some patriotic souls made a sport of shooting them down, but for every one they grounded, two replaced it.

Interestingly, martial law was predominately imposed over conservative areas of the country, leaving more liberal areas of the country relatively free. Doubtless this was done not only to keep potential secessionists under control, but to also keep liberals exposed to some degree of violence so that they will demand yet more government controls.

The dictator also limited each household to only one hunting rifle and a purchase limit of twenty-five rounds per year. Additionally, all handguns were confiscated and burned to joyous rioting in public squares across the country. The sales tax on all guns and ammunition increased dramatically to 90%.

The Supreme Court upheld these restrictions as constitutional, holding that the Second Amendment merely guaranteed access to a single firearm for self-protection, not to multiple guns or to certain types of firearms. The unanimous Court went so far as to suggest that the government could limit gun possession to the muzzleloader of the 18th century if it wanted to. This suggestion hardly went unnoticed in the years ahead.

To no one's great surprise, some started openly inciting secession in the face of such tyranny but, again to the surprise of no one, they were summarily executed for treason without judge or jury. Those who had foolishly signed the 2012 secession petition were arrested and held indefinitely without trial or bond. At the same time, however, the increase of Mexican nationalism among our Hispanic population and cries for reunification with their mother country went unpunished, likely out of fear of offending a large political constituency.

The dictator also declared religiosity—a belief in God, absolute truth, sin and need for repentance—a mental illness. Not only were those diagnosed with such an illness prohibited from owning guns, but they were prohibited from giving their children religious instruction. Such indoctrination was left to "neutral" world religion classes at school which taught that the only objective truth is the greatest amount of happiness for the greatest number of people. Employers and schools were required to mandate counseling for those diagnosed with this "mental disorder," and those who refused treatment and rehabilitation were dismissed.

I happened to own several rifles and handguns, and I also happened to be diagnosed (in abstentia, as I never appeared for my evaluation) with religiosity. In order to avoid having to turn in my firearms, however, I reported them stolen after burying them under the sandbox in the backyard. Oddly, they never asked why a middle-aged man with no children at home needed a brand-new sandbox, but I wasn't going to point out the obvious to them.

I attempted to impeach the president for his

measures which had no basis in either statute or the constitution, but the articles of impeachment were never debated. Only six congressmen joined me in my effort, the remaining remnant of the newly formed, but now newly dying, Liberty Party. The entitlement crises and the rise of the dictator made our freedom from government platform quite unpopular, forcing us to maintain a large security presence when we went out in public.

Congress, during this crises, became irrelevant, powerless, and emasculated. The president disregarded them entirely, assuming the inherent constitutional authority to legislate for the general welfare of the country. His logic was democratically unassailable—it was, he proclaimed, immoral for the nationwide majority that elected him to be thwarted by the much smaller majorities that elected those in Congress. The Supreme Court, of course, upheld this usurpation of authority.

The Constitution, however, envisioned the president as an executive, not a legislator. I denounced the Court's decision on the House floor with the following quote from Daniel Webster: "The contest, for all ages, has been to rescue liberty from the grasp of executive power. Through all this history of the contest for liberty, executive power has been regarded as a lion which must be caged. It has been dreaded, uniformly, always dreaded, as the great source of its danger."

Tragically, Americans forgot that the fundamental lesson of human history is that freedom and the protection of God–given unalienable rights are not the norm but the exception. Democracies are fleeting, and America was hardly immune to the historic reality that all republics have eventually dissolved into dictatorships.

In an attempt to postpone this inevitability, the Founding Generation established a written federal constitution with grants of limited, enumerated powers and counteracting checks and balances. In crafting the nature of the executive branch, the the Constitution bestowed on the President twelve powers:

1. He may exercise a qualified veto.
2. He shall be Commander in Chief.
3. He may require the written opinion of cabinet members.
4. He shall have power to grant pardons.
5. He shall have power, by and with the advice and consent of two–thirds of the Senate, to make treaties.
6. He shall nominate, and by and with the advice

and consent of the Senate, shall appoint ambassadors, judges, and all other officers of the United States, and shall have power to fill vacancies that may occur during a Senate recess.

7. He shall give Congress the state of the Union and recommend to their consideration such measures as he shall judge necessary and expedient.

8. He may, on extraordinary occasions, convene both Houses, or either of them.

9. He may, in case of disagreement between both Houses, with respect to the time of adjournment, adjourn them to such time as he shall think proper.

10.He shall receive ambassadors and other public ministers.

11.He shall take care that the laws be faithfully executed.

12.He shall commission all the officers of the United States.

That's it—only twelve grants of authority, none of which involve implementing one's own domestic policy agenda. The president's sole responsibility towards legislation was to "take care that the laws be faithfully executed." Those who drafted the

Constitution saw the president merely as an institution for carrying the will of the legislature into effect. Congress was to make the laws, the president to simply enforced them.

Ironically, it was the very congressional buying of votes by making political promises that lead to its own impotency. For when Washington promises to solve all our problems for us but fails to do anything but bicker, the electorate becomes ripe for a political savior who promises that, "If Congress won't act, I will." It is simple supply and demand—the electorate wants their Uncle Sugar Daddy, and a single executive is in a far better position to provide their fix than 535 squabbling congressmen.

I must close for now. Please know that I am praying for you constantly in these uncertain times as nuclear war appears imminent. I miss you terribly and hope to see you soon, but more on that later.

> Your affectionate grandfather,
> Col. Peter Iossi

LETTER XIV

MY DEAREST GRANDCHILDREN,

There is, so far, no indication that nuclear war has engulfed the North American continent. The reformed Mexican government has reached a peace treaty with the Pacific States of America and has withdrawn to a newly-established boundary line thirty miles south of Los Angeles. If they are going to exact revenge on the PSA for the extinction of their capital and most populous city, they're in no hurry to do so. Of course, the Mexicans waited nearly two-hundred years to recover the land they lost in the First Mexican-American War, so they have proven that they can wait until their enemy is sufficiently weakened.

The Mexicans have informed our leadership, and

our military intelligence has confirmed, that they have quickly accumulated a sufficient stock pile of both short-range and long-range nuclear warheads. They have announced, however, that they will only use them in response to a first strike from us. They apparently (and mistakenly) believe our propaganda that we have a vast, modern, and fully functioning nuclear arsenal that is more than ready and willing to annihilate every square inch of Mexican territory. Even if they suspected the truth, however, gambling in a nuclear standoff is never a smart thing to do.

So now the only active front with the Mexicans remains the battle for Texas, and it appears, at least for now, to remain a conventional war. And though my informants tell me that we are currently in peace negotiations with Mexico on how to divide Texas in half, our forces continue to clash on a daily basis as each side attempts to gain the upper hand. Neither side appears able to win this war of attrition, but so far neither side is willing to stop trying either.

No doubt our position is complicated by the fact that our interim president was the governor of Texas. He will have a very hard time agreeing to any partition of his home state, especially if his 1,500 acre ranch ends up on the Mexican side of the border as it is currently. His cattle have long since been butchered by the Mexicans, who used his house as their headquarters until our president gave the order to blow it up. Now all that is left is dirt, grass, and a few streams, but the property, which has been in his family for generations, has tremendous sentimental value to him.

Did you know that our president had the honor of being personally attacked by the dictator when, as governor, he ran against him in 2032 on the Liberty Party ticket? Though the Liberty Party didn't qualify for a seat at any of the presidential debates, the dictator invited our president as a show of his magnanimity. But during the debate the dictator became increasingly frustrated at being publicly challenged and, eventually losing any resemblance of self-control, tackled our president. The melee, unfortunately, was cut short as the secret service quickly intervened and whisked the dictator off stage before our president could fight back.

But despite such a childish display of pride and arrogance on national television, the dictator won reelection with an unbelievable 99% of the vote in every single congressional district, including my own. To make it even more unbelievable, no other presidential candidate received a single vote as the remaining one percent, apparently, did not vote for president. Though obviously rigged, no one was able to mount a successful legal challenge in court.

I managed to retain my seat in Congress, along with a paltry four other members of the Liberty Party. We were a dying breed, becoming little more than a voice crying out in the wilderness as the country devoured itself. Having flirted with socialism for the past century, Americans now fully embraced public ownership of private enterprise as the only way to ensure "equality," "fairness," and "shared sacrifice."

Entire industries such as gas, oil, mining, timber, agriculture and livestock, transportation, and supermarkets were nationalized because it was unfair that they should profit off of the basic necessities of others. Fortune 500 companies were also nationalized because, the dictator explained, they had grown rich at the expense of the poor and needed to be brought down to size. All other companies were required to have a Shared Sacrifice (SS) agent as the chairman of their board of directors.

In order to continue to fund the entitlement state, the dictator imposed a 100% tax on incomes over $50,000, arguing that it was blatantly unfair for some to make more than others. He also imposed a 100% death tax on estates over $50,000 because it was unconscionable for some to inherit money by the simple accident of birth into a "rich" family. He called it a nail in the coffin of the aristocratic landed gentry.

The dictator seized homes worth over $1 million and gave them to the homeless. He then confiscated homes between $200,000 and $1 million and rented them back to their previous owners at exorbitant rates.

Ironically, the dictator, never finding enough money to steal to fund his government programs, outlawed abortions in order to encourage the production of future taxpayers. After all, he agued, America may not have been in such financial woes had 75 million Americans not been aborted in the nearly 60 years since Roe v. Wade. This was a line too far for the Supreme Court, who in a five-four decision ruled that such an edict violated the right to privacy. The dictator merely ignored them, paraphrasing President Andrew Jackson that "the court has made its decision, now let it enforce it." They couldn't, and they didn't.

Euthanasia became a commonplace means of rationing health care costs throughout the nationalized health care industry. At first it was done simply by denying critical care, but it was never efficient or quick enough to meet the bottom line. So by the dictator's second term, patients were routinely given the needle if the cost of their care exceeded their predetermined but undisclosed lifetime allotment based on age, life expectancy, health risks, and other factors. Family members, of course, were kept in the dark, mislead by medical staff that their loved ones had been transferred, or was unable to receive visitors, or, worse of all, that they no longer wanted to see them.

Because a belief in God and an Absolute Truth to which men and nations alike are held to account was seen as a threat to the state, the dictator banned those with the "mental illness" of religiosity from the public arena. After all, he argued, it is impossible for them to be a loyal citizen when their loyalty lies with God rather than the state. Henceforth they were no longer eligible to serve in the military, public education, or to hold any elected or appointed public office.

Going a step further, the dictator held that in order to receive government benefits or employment, one had to first take the Loyalty Oath as follows: "I pledge my unfailing and undivided loyalty to the president, who is the savior of his country and the sole arbitrator of virtue and shared sacrifice." Since one's health care was dependent on taking the oath, millions sighed their resignation as they publicly swore their fidelity to the dictator.

Needless to say, I was out of a job, along with the vast majority of the rest of the country. All the measures taken by the dictator only increased the country's economic misery rather than elevate it. By 2033, unemployment levels had reached 55% as the economy shrunk to pre-1976 levels. There were far too few taxpayers supporting far too many dependents, and there wasn't enough money to confiscate to make the balance sheets even.

When an entitlement state cannot borrow money, print money, confiscate money, or ration money, it collapses on itself. The dictator was assassinated on the very day he announced that massive cuts would have to be made to entitlement spending, and national chaos ensued shortly thereafter. In declaring nationwide martial law, the dictator's vice-president also limited gun rights to muzzleloaders, threatening that violators would be shot on sight.

The nation had finally had enough; not necessarily with the entitlement state, but with the police state. Secession, once it arrived in early 2034, became a largely peaceful mass exodus. I was asked by our future president to serve on a five-member secret committee to draft a Declaration of Independence.

Borrowing the preamble from the original, the new document justified secession by reciting "a long train of abuses and usurpations" that sought to bring us "under absolute despotism."

The new Declaration was initially agreed to by the governors of eight states—Mississippi, Alabama, Texas, Oklahoma, Kansas, Nebraska, Utah, and Montana. They announced the Declaration of Independence, forwarded it for ratification to state conventions, mobilized their national guard units, and asked for a million new recruits.

The response was overwhelming. Within a span of twenty-four hours, two million recruits joined the new army, eight new states—Tennessee, Kentucky, Louisiana, Indiana, South and North Dakota, Wyoming, and Arizona—joined the movement, and U.S. military units in the seceding states defected. Iowa, Missouri, Arkansas, Colorado, Nevada, New Mexico, and San Diego would later join the new nation.

Once started, the remaining dominos quickly followed. By the end of the week, Maine, New Hampshire, Vermont, and northern New York state joined Canada rather than remain in the United States. Florida declared itself a republic, and most of the West Coast formed itself as the Pacific States of

America. Unfortunately, not all dominos fell of their own free will as China seized Hawaii while simultaneously swallowing Taiwan and the Philippines, and Russia completed its take over of Alaska by annexing the remaining 35% of the state.

The United States government, though largely powerless to stem the flood, did find enough money to send in troops to brutally crush secessionist movements in West Virginia, Georgia, South Carolina, western Virginia and North Carolina, and southern Ohio and Illinois. Mostly, however, the secession was bloodless; all sides happy to see the others go.

It was in the midst of this national upheaval that Mexico seized the opportunity to reclaim its long lost land. Mexican nationalism had been on the rise for over a decade among America's Hispanic population, and as the nation fell apart around them they clamored for Mexican intervention. But when Mexico did invade and sought to enlist them as a sixth column, most fled to safer regions as they remember what life was like back in the old country.

Though I had just been elected to serve in our new country's constitutional convention when Mexico invaded, I quickly resigned to accept the rank of colonel in the newly formed marine corp. By the time we were ready to meet our enemy in combat, they had already captured Arizona, New Mexico, and large portions of Colorado, Utah, and Nevada. Cut off from the rest of us, San Diego, the Central Valley of California, the Sierra Nevada, and northern Nevada and Utah formed the Republic of California and fought (unsuccessfully) to withstand the Mexican onslaught.

As I previously wrote you, my regiment had been sent to try to drive Mexican forces out of Colorado and, eventually, Utah. Unfortunately, we were outnumbered and faced a much better prepared and seasoned fighting force. And now I rot in prison with what is left of my regiment.

But perhaps not for long, as the tuberculosis epidemic has ended with the coming of spring and my men are returning to fighting strength. Additionally, we have miraculously been able to build up a small stash of weapons, including a few sticks of dynamite. It is our hope, once summer arrives, to be able to fight our way back to you.

But until then, we must be patient. Please know that I pray for you continuously, and that I hope to write (or see you) soon.

Your affectionate grandfather,

Col. Peter Iossi

LETTER XV

MY DEAREST GRANDCHILDREN,

This will be my last letter to you before I hopefully see you face to face. Summer has officially come, the snow has melted, and the evening temperatures are quite comfortable. Perfect weather for traveling cross-country on foot.

We have been prisoners of war for over a year now, and there sadly appears no end in sight. Our country has finally settled on a border with Mexico (our president lost his ranch), but the status of prisoners of war has been left unresolved. With our soldiers heading home from the front and peace negotiators set to discuss our fate in December, we fear that we may not survive another six months in here. And if negotiations drag on, we will likely not make it through another winter.

We are healthy, we have weapons, and we have the element of surprise. Unfortunately, our guards outnumber us, outgun us, and they control the only way out. Revolt against such odds would be foolish, except for the fact that we have help from the outside. A nearby remnant of a company of Colorado Guardsmen are willing to blow up the watch towers and attack the front gate at the same time we attack from within. Victory is still not guaranteed, nothing in life is, but the risk must be taken.

If successful, we should be home by Labor Day and the start of the football season. If not, however, I hope my letters have helped explain to you the sins of the past so that your generation can be spared repeating them in the future. The task now belongs to you to create a new country, free from the specter of statism and socialism.

We did not arrive at this moment in history by accident or happenstance. We did not suddenly wake up one morning to find ourselves in a semi-communist republic. Our journey to this point was generations in the making and spanned over a hundred years. We got here because we no longer feared government but surrendered to the belief that it must provide us with benefits and privileges.

This belief in government-provided fairness and financial security was indoctrinated in our youth by our education systems and reinforced by the liberal media and entertainment industries. It was fueled by the breakdown of the family and met little resistance as society grew increasingly secular and immoral. Freedom died culturally long before it died electorally.

A society must never forget that government is a necessary evil established to preserve man's natural and unalienable right to life, liberty, and property. Government fulfills this task by providing for the national defense and creation of a criminal and civil justice system.

Government, however, runs the risk of violating its mission when it seeks to go beyond this limited role and legislate for the "general welfare." When it seeks to regulate man's enjoyment of his natural rights rather than serve as an impartial arbitrator of them, it must satisfy the presumption of liberty— the most local form of democratic government feasible that addresses a necessary public interest by using the least restrictive means available which do not deprive one of his rights in order to give to them to another (i.e., redistribution of wealth or forced equality of outcomes).

The modern welfare, administrative, social-democratic state cannot govern, however, without violating man's natural rights. It denies any notion of individual sovereignty or God-given freedoms, it perverts rights into man-made entitlements dispersed at the pleasure of the state, and legalized robbery becomes a way of life as the only way it can give to B is by first stealing from A.

It is the antithesis of liberty, and no amount of reform can make it otherwise. There can be no middle ground or accommodation between the two; one can only exist at the expense of the other. Either the state is the servant of the individual, or the individual is the servant of the state.

Socialism bankrupts the national soul, and then it bankrupts the nation. It cannot be tamed or compromised with, only renounced in all its forms. Once it takes hold, it is nearly impossible for a society to voluntarily relinquish it. Because they will often continue to worship it even after it destroys them, it would be far better for a society to never flirt with socialism to begin with.

To that end, there are six principles that a society must never negotiate or abandon. The first is federalism—a central government of limited, constitutionally enumerated powers. The history lesson of the ages is that centralized power is the single greatest threat to individual liberty, and for that reason our new central government must be denied any authority to interfere with a state's domestic policy. Activities such as education, workplace regulations, manufacturing, agriculture, and crime that occur within the boundaries of a single state should be off limits to the federal government.

Second, a balanced budget must be constitutionally demanded of the new government. Additionally, a two-thirds majority of both houses of the legislature should be required to both raise taxes and the debt ceiling. Third, the new constitution must prohibit lawmaking by unelected bureaucrats by requiring that all such regulations be approved by the legislature before they take affect and that the benefits of such regulations outweigh the costs.

Fourth, society must never lose sight of the fact that legal plunder—using the law to take from one person what belongs to them, and giving it to others to whom it does not belong—is morally repugnant and unconscionable. It is a form of slavery, both to those who labor for others and to those who become dependent on such labor. The new constitution, therefore, should prohibit the subsidization of any individual, organization, business, industry, or state.

Fifth, society must demand a wall of separation between the economy and the state in which the government will not seek to, directly or indirectly, intervene, manipulate, or otherwise control the economy. It must not favor, save, protect, or "invest in" certain industries or companies, nor attempt to make things—whether jobs, college education, health insurance, secure retirement, and homes—more affordable and universal than they would otherwise be in the free market.

Such government planning only slows economic growth by subsidizing some consumers and producers at the expense of others. Central planning is no more successful or moral when practiced by democratic elites managing a mixed economy than by socialists in a communist dictatorship.

Sixth and finally, a society must never forget that man's unalienable right to own a firearm predates any constitution. It is a natural right of individual sovereignty to have the weapons available to protect himself against both criminals and tyranny alike. By removing any resistance to evil men, gun control merely invites the violence which it was intended to prevent.

If our new country does not take these tenants to

heart, it is bound to eventually become the dictatorship it just fled. It may take a hundred years or even two-hundred, but without these moral and constitutional safeguards, liberty will remain a fleeting and unsustainable dream.

It is my hope to join you soon as we seek to provide stronger protections for freedom as we create a new country. Look for my coming around Labor Day, when we will finally be able to embrace and laugh and cry, mourn and rejoice together. But if that is not the will of Providence, always remember that you are loved and that I will be anxiously awaiting your homecoming on that far heavenly shore.

With my everlasting love until we meet again.

Your affectionate grandfather,

Col. Peter Iossi

AUTHOR'S NOTE

The events depicted in this novel—which were plotted before the 2012 election and with a different outcome hoped for—are only one of many possible scenarios that may take place in America's future. Some, all, none, or variations of these tragedies—which intentionally excluded external threats—may occur within or beyond the timeframe used in the story. They are not intended to be predictions, but merely warnings.

The only certain thing is that America's debt is unsustainable and, at some point, the Ponzi scheme will come to a terrifying end. However it unfolds, the collapse of America will not have a happy ending. That story does not have to be told, but will only be avoided if a different one is begun today. That will only occur if the debt ceiling is not raised and the federal government is forced to live within its means.

Revenue (in the trillions of dollars) will still come in to keep the government operating and prevent a shutdown, but it will force America to live within a balanced budget. Republicans in the House could obtain a balanced budget overnight simply by refusing to raise the debt ceiling one more time.

They don't need a balanced budget amendment or

a majority in the Senate and control of the White House to accomplish this goal; all they need to do is just say no. To date, however, they have yet to show the fortitude to do so, and with each failure of responsibility America's rendezvous with economic and societal collapse becomes increasingly inevitable.

COMING NOVEMBER 2013:

JULIA'S

CHRISTMAS

CAROL

By Nathan W. Tucker

During the 2012 U.S. presidential election, the Obama campaign released the Life of Julia, a slideshow which chronicled the life of a woman as she lived off of the cradle-to-grave welfare state. This year she encounters the Ghosts of Christmases Past, Present, and Future on her journey towards redemption. Think Charles Dickens meets Henry Hazlitt.